David sighed as he glanced sideways.

His gaze rested on the cameo-like perfection of Laura's profile. If only he knew that he would wake up at some point and find that this was all a dream, he could sit back and enjoy it!

But Laura was a flesh-and-blood woman, and therein lay the real danger. It would be only too easy to be carried away by her warmth and beauty, but at what cost to his peace of mind? How could he betray Kate by allowing another woman into his mind and into his life?

Dear Reader

One of the joys of writing is the opportunity it gives
you to create new characters, so you can imagine my
delight when I was asked to create a whole town!

Yewdale is purely the product of my imagination but
during the course of writing this series the characters
who live there became very real to me. Gruff old
Isaac Shepherd, nosy Marion Rimmer, the Jackson
family with their frequent crises... I would sit down at
the typewriter each morning, eager to discover what
was happening in their lives.

Writing this series has been quite simply a delight. I
have had the pleasure of not only bringing together
each couple and watching them fall in love, but of
seeing how their lives were enriched by the people
around them. I hope that you enjoy reading the books
as much as I have enjoyed writing them.

My very best wishes to you.

Jennifer Taylor

OUR NEW
MUMMY

BY
JENNIFER TAYLOR

MILLS & BOON®

First published in Great Britain 1999
Harlequin Mills & Boon Limited,
Eton House, 18-24 Paradise Road, Richmond, Surrey TW9 1SR

© Jennifer Taylor 1999

ISBN 0 263 81699 0

Set in Times Roman 10½ on 12 pt.
03-9906-52026-D

Printed and bound in Spain
by Litografía Rosés S.A., Barcelona

CHAPTER ONE

'FOR the third and last time, we'll be fine!' Dr David Ross looked at his two partners. It was obvious that one of them at least still wasn't convinced. 'Sam and I can manage perfectly well without you for a couple of days,' he repeated with weary patience.

'Are you sure, David? It just seems awful, James and me both going off like this...' Elizabeth Allen tailed off as David raised his eyes in exasperation.

'You're only going to miss tonight's surgery. This practice isn't going to grind to a halt because of that!' David turned to the younger man imploringly. 'Can't you convince this fiancée of yours that Sam and I are perfectly able—not to mention *willing*—to cope while you visit your parents, James?'

'I've tried, believe me, but you know what a worry-boots Beth can be. Look how long it took me to convince her that the people in this town were safe in my hands!' James Sinclair laughed affectionately as Elizabeth gasped in outrage. He smiled at her, his face full of tender amusement. 'Come on, darling, admit it—you were worried sick that I was going to cause problems when I first arrived here.'

'And can you blame me? Look at the disruption you've caused already by making me fall in love with you!' Elizabeth retorted, returning his smile with an equally adoring one of her own.

'I think you're both making a lot of fuss about nothing.' David got up from his desk and went to the win-

5

dow, trying to ignore the pang he felt at the couple's obvious happiness.

Like everyone else in the small Cumbrian town of Yewdale, he was thrilled about their impending marriage, but at times he couldn't help feeling a certain envy for what they had and what he had lost when his wife, Kate, had died just over a year before. However, he refused to let them guess how he was feeling as he turned to them now with a smile.

'Look, you idiots, you're only going to London for the weekend. Now, as far as I can foretell, there won't be an outbreak of the Black Death around here. However, I promise on my honour to phone you if there is. London isn't the other side of the world, in case you've forgotten. So, please, get yourselves out of here and let the rest of us get on with some work!'

Elizabeth laughed ruefully. 'You're right. It is only for a couple of days after all, and I doubt anything momentous can happen in that time! I must be getting cold feet at the thought of meeting my future in-laws for the first time.'

'Beth, darling, they'll love you! They couldn't do anything else. Now, I think we should do exactly as we've been told to and get out of here.' James put both hands on his fiancée's shoulders and steered her towards the door. He paused briefly to glance back. 'Thanks, David. I owe you one for this.'

'I'll keep you to that!' David retorted jokingly, as they finally left. Picking up a pen, he returned to the stack of paperwork which needed attending to, but after a moment realised that his mind wasn't really on the task. He sighed as he leaned back in the chair. He felt restless and on edge, and it had been happening a lot lately. He seemed to have reached a point in his life where there was nothing to aim for any more.

What had happened to that wonderful feeling of expectancy each day had once brought? He could barely recall how it had felt to wake up looking forward to a new day.

'David…have you got a moment?' Eileen Pierce, the receptionist, popped her head round the door. David cut short his introspection as he beckoned the middle-aged woman into the room.

'Of course, Eileen. What's wrong?'

'I've got Marie Rogerson on the phone. Evidently her husband isn't well, and she wants to know if someone can go out to see him.' Eileen sighed.

'Sam went out on a couple of calls after surgery. He wasn't expecting to be away long but he rang about half an hour ago to say that he was at Yewthwaite Farm, waiting for an ambulance to get there. Apparently, old Mrs Walsh has had a fall and he thinks her hip is broken. I could ring him back and ask him to go over to the Rogersons' house, but I wasn't sure that was what you'd want me to do.'

'No, best leave Sam where he is. It would take him a good half-hour to get back from Yewthwaite Farm even if he leaves right away, and I'd prefer him to stay there until the ambulance arrives in case of any problems. I'll go and take a look at Cyril Rogerson myself. Tell his wife I'm on my way, will you, Eileen, please?'

It was a glorious afternoon when David drove out of the surgery gates five minutes later. It was only the end of May but the weather had been marvellous for the past couple of weeks. It had brought an influx of early tourists into the town so traffic was heavy as he made his way through the narrow streets.

David's mind went back to the first time he'd seen the town as he crawled along in the stream of traffic. Ten years ago he and Kate had come to Yewdale as visitors, drawn here by the stunning scenery in this part of the world. They had been immediately smitten by the charm of the town, with its quaintly old-fashioned shops and grey stone houses. When the opportunity had arisen a short time later for David to work here, he'd jumped at the chance.

Elizabeth's father, Charles Allen, had taken him on as a junior partner in those days. Elizabeth had been away at medical school and it hadn't been certain if she'd return to Yewdale to work once she qualified.

In the event, she had come back but there had been more than enough work for the three of them. The area they'd covered was extensive, comprising not only the town itself but the outlying farms as well. There had been plenty to keep them busy, sufficient to make it hard to manage even with the help of their locum, Sam O'Neill. Then Charles Allen had a heart attack and was forced to retire at the beginning of the year.

They'd advertised for a third partner and had taken on James Sinclair almost two months ago now. It had been a rather rocky ride at first because Elizabeth hadn't seemed to take to James at all. Now David smiled as he thought about how things had worked out.

Elizabeth and James were to be married in September, proof that any doubts she'd had about their new partner had definitely been ironed out! Things were settling back into some degree of normality after all the upheavals, which made it harder than ever to understand why he felt so restless.

What was he looking for? he wondered suddenly. He couldn't imagine working anywhere else so that couldn't be the problem. Maybe it was the fact that there had been such a gap in his life since Kate died and yet he couldn't imagine anyone ever filling it. He might envy his partners a little but he wasn't looking for love again. Just the thought of another woman in his life made him feel guilty, as though he'd be betraying Kate and everything they'd had.

David's mouth thinned at the thought as he pulled up in front of the Rogersons' neat stone cottage. Reaching across the seat for his case, he caught a glimpse of himself in the rear-view mirror and nearly laughed out loud as he took stock of the silver threads laced through his dark brown hair and the lines etched around his grey eyes.

Who was he kidding? He was forty-three years old, with three children and a job that demanded most of his waking time. What woman in her right mind would give him a second glance?

'Right, Cyril, if you'd just like to slip your shirt back on again.' David rolled up his stethoscope and popped it back into his case as Cyril Rogerson slowly started getting dressed.

'What do you think it is, Dr Ross? It just isn't like Cyril to be poorly like this.' Marie Rogerson sounded worried as she helped her husband slip his arms into a chunky-knit cardigan then got him settled in a chair by the fireplace. Despite how mild it was that day, there was a fire burning in the grate. It made the room incredibly hot and stuffy but Cyril immediately huddled towards the blaze.

'To be honest, Marie, I'm not sure what's wrong with Cyril. His chest is clear enough and his heart is as sound as a bell so there's nothing to worry about in that respect.' David turned to the older man. 'I had a look at your notes before I came, Cyril, and, as Marie says, you've hardly been a regular visitor to the surgery over the years.'

'Aye, that's right enough, Dr Ross. Most I ever suffer from is a touch of hay fever. Oh, and I had a bad throat a few weeks back—caught a chill when I went fishing with my grandson while we were staying in Norwich with our Sarah. But that all cleared up fast enough,' Cyril added, sounding exhausted.

David studied him in concern. Cyril had never been a heavily built man but it was obvious that he'd lost a lot of weight recently because his clothes were hanging on him. David frowned as he searched for the missing link that would help him discover what the problem was. 'And you say that you've been vomiting in the past couple of days?'

'The odd time or two.'

'The odd time, indeed!' Marie Rogerson folded her arms across her ample bosom and glared at her husband. 'You tell Dr Ross the truth now, Cyril, as how you've barely touched a thing these past three days because every time you try to eat you're sick.' She turned to David. 'That's why I insisted on calling you, Dr Ross. Cyril kept saying as it was just a bit of a tummy bug and not to make a fuss, but he can't keep on like this!'

'Indeed, he can't, Marie. I can see for myself that he's lost quite a bit of weight recently,' David agreed. 'I suppose it's possible that you've contracted some sort of food poisoning. I know you work at the pottery and I assume you eat in the canteen there. Has anyone else been ill, do you know?'

Cyril shook his head. 'Not as I recall, but, of course,

I wouldn't know if any of the office staff have been off. With me being on the shop floor, I don't always see everyone from upstairs.'

'You're in charge of firing the china, aren't you, Cyril?' David continued thoughtfully.

'Yes, that's right. We're coming up to our busiest time, too, getting stocked up ready for the tourists. And we've just landed an order for some big shop down in London as well. Taken a real fancy to some of our tableware, they have,' Cyril added proudly. 'We've all been working flat out to get it ready. Frankly, Dr Ross, I can't afford to be off sick at the moment. It couldn't have come at a worse time.'

'Is there any chance that the chemicals you're using might have affected you? Are you using anything new in the production process, do you know?' David queried, trying a new track to get to the root of Cyril's problem.

'Not so far as I know. No, it's probably just a bit of food poisoning, like you said. I had a pasty in the canteen the other day and it didn't taste all that brilliant. Maybe it was that.'

'Maybe,' David agreed, but he couldn't shake off the feeling that there might be rather more to Cyril's problem than a mild case of food poisoning. 'Anyway, what I want you to do is to avoid eating anything for the next twenty-four hours, although you must drink plenty so you don't become dehydrated. That should give your system time to get rid of whatever it is that's affecting it. But if you don't feel any better in a couple of days then you're to come into the surgery. Understand?'

'Right, Dr Ross. I'll do as you say. But I expect I'll be right as rain in a day or so,' Cyril added valiantly.

David drove straight back to the surgery after he left the Rogersons' house as there wasn't time to call home before his evening appointments started. He went to his room and dialled his home phone number, waiting patiently for one of the children to answer.

Mike picked it up at the tenth ring, raising his voice to carry over the heavy beat of background rock music. 'Hello?'

'Mike, it's me. I'm just checking to see you're OK. I had to go out on a call so I didn't have time to pop in this afternoon. Is Emily all right?' he asked his seventeen-year-old son.

'Yeah, she's fine. She's over at Laura's. I suppose you want me to get tea ready. It'll have to be pizza, though, 'cos I've got a history essay which has to be in first thing Monday morning, and it'll take me the whole weekend to get it finished!'

'Yes, that's fine. Don't worry about it.' David curbed the urge to ask his son why he'd left writing the essay until the very last moment. Schoolwork—especially Mike's failed GCSEs, which he was having to resit— was a sore point, even though David knew that the boy wasn't really to blame for his dismal results. Kate's illness had been hard on all of them, and it was little wonder that Mike hadn't been able to concentrate on his work as he should have done.

He exchanged another few words with Mike then hung up, realising only as he put the phone down what Mike had said about Emily being at Laura's house. Try as he may, David couldn't remember his eight-year-old daughter ever mentioning a friend by that name.

It was gone seven when David finally arrived home that night. He slammed the car door, wondering if it was his imagination that the engine had sounded rather rough coming up the lane. He'd had his foot right to the floor yet the car had only just made it up the incline.

He sighed as he opened the front door. The car was well overdue for a service and he'd have to get it in to the garage soon otherwise he could find himself stranded, not a pleasant prospect in view of the area he covered during a day's work!

Emily was sprawled across the living-room floor, crayoning a picture, when he went in. She jumped up and ran to him, hanging around his neck like a little monkey as he swung her up into the air.

She was so like Kate that David felt a lump come to his throat. She had the same thick black curls, the same warm brown eyes and dazzling smile—even the same loving nature as her mother had had. Emily loved everyone and wanted them to be happy, and it was hard not to feel that way with her around.

'We had pizza for tea and we saved you a piece. I thought you'd be home when I got back from school though, Daddy. You said you would be this morning.'

'I had to go out to see someone, poppet. Sorry.' David gave her a quick hug then set her down. He flopped into a chair with a groan of relief. 'Oh, it's good to be home! Come on, tell me what you've been up to today. How was school?'

'Fine.' Emily sat on the arm of the chair, her arm looped around David's neck. 'We had reading and art this morning, then PE. Chloe Jackson came into school this afternoon to see everyone, and she hasn't got any hair. Some of the boys laughed at her but I told them off because it isn't fair when she's been ill. Mrs Johnson told us it was the drugs that have made

Chloe's hair fall out and that it will grow again soon. Will it, though, Daddy?'

Emily sounded worried and David smiled reassuringly. 'Of course it will, darling. And your teacher was quite right because it *was* the drugs which made Chloe's hair fall out. She had leukaemia, you see, and she needed a lot of very powerful drugs to make her better.'

'Yes, that's what Laura said.' Emily got off her perch and lay on the floor again to resume her crayoning.

'Did she?' David frowned. 'Funny, I don't recall you mentioning anyone called Laura before. Is she new around here?' He glanced round as the doorbell rang and half rose from his chair before Mike shouted that he'd answer it.

'Uh-huh. She only moved in a few weeks ago.' Emily carefully selected another crayon, her tongue caught between her teeth as she started to colour in the grass with a vivid lime green.

'I see. So where about does this Laura live? It must be close by if you were round at her house tonight, playing,' David said.

'Oh, very close. Right next door, in fact. It couldn't be better when we want to play, could it, Emily?'

David glanced round in surprise at the sound of the unfamiliar voice. He rose to his feet, wondering if it was just surprise at seeing a stranger in his house that had caused his heart to miss a beat. The woman gave a husky laugh as she came into the room and held out her hand.

'Hello, I'm Laura Mackenzie. I'm sorry if I startled you. I've moved in next door so I rather think that makes us neighbours as well as me being Emily's new playmate!'

David took her outstretched hand and was immediately struck by how small it was, but, then, there was a definite air of fragility about her—despite the way she was dressed!

His eyes widened as they swept from the untidy knot of blonde hair, precariously pinned to the top of her head, down to a perfect oval face whose dainty features bore not a trace of make-up but a good deal of buttercup-yellow paint splashes.

Her clothes consisted of a pair of denim dungarees worn with a red check shirt, both of which also showed copious evidence of the same yellow paint. The shirt was obviously a man's and far too large for her because she'd had to roll up the sleeves at least a dozen times to make them fit.

David couldn't help noticing how impossibly fragile her wrists looked as they poked out from the rolls of cloth. The combination of bulky denim and excess red check made it impossible to tell what shape the rest of her was, but he just *knew* there were lusciously feminine curves somewhere beneath the bizarre outfit.

He felt his body quicken with a speed that shocked him, and abruptly he let go of her hand, afraid that she'd guess the effect she'd had on him. 'I'm pleased to meet you, Ms Mackenzie,' he said stiffly, shocked by his instantaneous response to the woman.

'Ms Mackenzie?' She gave another of those husky laughs which made his skin prickle with heat. 'Oh, please, I can't bear that dreadful, neither-one-thing-nor-another title! It's *Miss* Mackenzie, or even *Dr* Mackenzie, if you prefer. But I'm really hoping that you'll make it Laura.'

Her beautiful blue eyes rose to his face and David felt as though someone had punched him ever so lightly in the solar plexus as she added softly, 'I'd like to think that we can be friends as well as neighbours, David.'

There was a moment when words seemed to escape him, a moment when he looked into Laura Mackenzie's eyes and hoped for all sorts of things—none of them befitting a respectable widower with three children! It took the sudden ringing of the telephone in the hall to bring him to his senses.

He gave Laura a quick smile, not trusting himself to give her a longer one in case his common sense got hijacked again. 'If you'll excuse me a moment, Miss...Laura,' he amended quickly as he saw her blonde brows rise reprovingly.

'Of course.' She moved aside so that he could pass her, but even from the relatively safe distance of several feet David caught the scent of her perfume. He hurried out into the hall, trying to ignore the way the blood was racing through his veins as he snatched up the receiver.

Saved by the bell! he thought with an attempt at humour because he was shocked by his response to the woman.

But saved from what? a small voice whispered. How could Laura Mackenzie present any sort of danger to him? And that, of course, was the sixty-four-thousand-dollar question!

CHAPTER TWO

'HELLO? Are you there, Dr Ross?'

David dragged his mind back to what was happening as he heard the anxious voice at the other end of the line. 'Yes, this is David Ross speaking. How can I help you?'

'It's Gary Morrison over at Rowbottom Farm. Anna has started with the baby. I've rung the midwife but she's out on another call and I didn't know what to do!'

'I see. Have you phoned for an ambulance?' David frowned. Surely the baby wasn't due yet? Anna worked at the local pottery, as so many people in Yewdale did. David had signed a form for her to claim her maternity entitlements only a few weeks earlier, and as far as he recalled her baby wasn't due for another month at least.

'Yes! I've just this minute rung them, only they say as it will be almost an hour before they can get an ambulance to us. The baby's on its way now, Dr Ross, this very minute! It wasn't due until the end of June, but Anna started having pains just after tea—' Gary broke off as there was a muffled shout in the background. He came back on the line, sounding more frantic than ever. 'Anna says as she can feel the baby's head now!'

'Right. Just try to stay calm, Gary. I'll be with you as soon as I can.' David checked his watch, mentally estimating how long it would take him to get to Rowbottom Farm. 'It should take me twenty minutes

17

at most, but in the meantime I want you to keep Anna
as calm as possible. Is she in bed?'

'No. I couldn't get her up the stairs—they're too
steep, you see. She's on the floor in the living room.'

'Then make sure that she's lying on something
warm, and pack some towels under her. Hopefully, I'll
get there before the baby arrives, but be ready in case
it beats me to it. Don't try to cut the cord or do anything other than keep the baby warm. Oh, and there
might be a thin membrane over its face when it's born
and you'll need to remove that straight away to help it
breathe.'

'Me? But I don't think...' Gary took a gulping
breath. 'Right you are, Doctor. But get here fast, won't
you?'

'I'll be there just as soon as I can. If you have any
problems ring me on my mobile. I'll keep it switched
on.' David gave Gary the number then wasted no more
time. Snatching up his case, he went back to the sitting-
room.

'I've got to go out. There's a bit of an emergency
over at Rowbottom Farm—a baby on its way rather
sooner than expected. Tell Mike I'll be as quick as I
can, will you, Emily? But I'm not sure how long it's
going to take.'

'Is there anything I can do?' Laura offered immediately.

'Thanks, but I've got it covered,' David knew his
tone was a shade too cool but he was having a hard
time coming to terms with the way he'd behaved before. How could he have felt such things for this
woman—a stranger? It made him feel guilty that he
should have responded the way he had to Laura. He'd

loved Kate so much, and yet all it took was a pretty woman smiling at him and he got all twisted up inside.

He swung round abruptly, made his way out of the house and got into his car, wondering only as he slipped the key into the ignition what Laura had wanted tonight. He hadn't stopped long enough to find out, but it was hardly the time to start worrying about it now!

He put his foot on the accelerator then cursed softly as the engine immediately cut out. He started it up again but once more the engine stalled the moment he tried to drive off. Reaching under the dashboard, he popped the bonnet release catch and got out hurriedly to see if he could spot what was wrong, but there didn't appear to be anything obviously amiss—to his eyes, at least.

'Problems?'

He swung round at the sound of that already familiar voice, feeling the heat pool in the pit of his stomach as he found Laura standing behind him. His instantaneous response to the sight of her annoyed him intensely so that his tone was brusque. 'Nothing I can't handle, thank you.'

Laura's brows rose as she caught the faint antagonism in his voice, but her tone remained as even as ever. 'Well, if you get stuck just give me a shout. I'll be happy to run you over to wherever it is you're going.'

She gave him the same warm smile she'd given him when she'd walked into his sitting-room a few minutes earlier, making David feel like the biggest boor going. What did it cost to be polite? he reproved himself sternly. It wasn't *her* fault he was acting so oddly!

'Thanks, I appreciate the offer,' he replied, and even managed a smile, then felt his pulse leap as Laura re-

turned it with a far more dazzling one. She turned and
made her way back through the gap in the hedge to her
own house, and David heard the sound of a door closing.

He took a deep breath, resolutely striving to keep his
mind on the job as he bent over the engine and began
poking around. However, after five minutes he was
forced to admit defeat. He had no idea what was wrong
with the car, which left him with an emergency on his
hands and no way of dealing with it. Unless...

Laura answered the door immediately, leaving David
with the distinct impression that she'd been waiting for
him to knock! He clamped down on the embarrassment
he felt at that thought, concentrating instead on the reason he was standing on her step, although he had to
admit that it wasn't easy to concentrate on anything
right then.

It might have been only a few minutes since Laura
had gone home, but in that short time she'd managed
to change out of the clothes she'd been wearing earlier.
David tried not to stare, but it was impossible not to
notice how well the beige jeans fitted her trim hips or
how enticingly the orange T-shirt clung to her rounded
breasts. Laura Mackenzie had curves, just as he'd suspected, and in all the right places. However, it didn't
help restore his equilibrium to realise he'd been right!

'About that offer you just made—is it still on?' he
asked quickly, deeming it safer to stick to what he'd
come for.

'Of course.' She took a set of keys from a hook
beside the door then pursed her lips and whistled, smiling as she saw his surprise. 'I'm afraid Peebody gets a
trifle neurotic if I leave him on his own for too long.

He hasn't quite grasped the idea that we'll be living here part of the time as well as in the flat.'

'Peebody—' David began, then broke off as he got his first glimpse of the owner of the name. His astonished eyes rose to Laura's amused ones and he heard her laugh.

'*This* is Peebody. He's part Irish Wolfhound, so I'm told, but don't let his size fool you. All the rest of him is pure coward!' Laura explained as the huge dog skidded to a halt beside her. He was the biggest dog David had ever seen, his huge grey head reaching way above Laura's waist. David didn't dare speculate how big the animal would be if it stood on its hind legs. Probably taller than him, and he was a good six feet in his socks!

David didn't say anything more as he followed Laura and the dog round to the front of the cottage, and then he got yet another shock. Not for Laura Mackenzie some smart saloon or snazzy little sports car. The vehicle she drove was a Land Rover, and one which didn't look as though it had even seen better days let alone could remember them.

David shot a horrified glance at the khaki-rust paintwork. Maybe it wasn't too late to find some other form of transport, he thought desperately, then sighed as he opened the creaking door. Who was he kidding? It was this or nothing because he had to get to Rowbottom Farm, although whether he'd make it in one piece was open to speculation.

Laura seemed blissfully unaware of his thoughts as she urged the dog into the back and climbed behind the wheel. She slid the key into the ignition, smiling as the engine responded with a sweet purr. 'Daisy might not look much but she's never let me down yet. Right, which way, then?'

She turned to David, a trace of the smile lingering on her lips so that he had great difficulty remembering where they were going let alone which direction they should take. He turned to stare out of the window, praying that Laura wouldn't guess how he was feeling—although it seemed unlikely. Frankly, *he* had no idea how he felt so how on earth could she work it out?

'Straight through town and out towards Newthwaite. I'll have to direct you once we get out into the open as the farm is a bit off the beaten track,' he explained, pleased to hear that his voice sounded almost normal.

'Fine. Hold tight.' Laura slipped the vehicle into gear and pulled out into the lane, putting her foot down as soon as they got onto the main road. David stared through the windscreen, watching the hedges and trees rushing past. The evening was drawing in and the fading daylight had a surreal quality to it, faintly blue and dreamlike...but, then, didn't it feel as though he had stepped right into the middle of some crazy dream?

He sighed as he glanced sideways, his gaze resting on the cameo-like perfection of Laura's profile. If only he knew that he would wake up at some point and find that this was all a dream, he could sit back and enjoy it!

But Laura was a flesh-and-blood woman, and therein lay the real danger. It would be only too easy to be carried away by her warmth and beauty, but at what cost to his peace of mind? How could he betray Kate by allowing another woman into his mind and into his life?

They drove in silence for the first ten minutes or so. David had his own thoughts to deal with and Laura was concentrating on the road. They'd left Yewdale behind and were heading out into the open country when Laura suddenly sighed.

'It's so beautiful here. I can't believe my luck at being able to live here even if it is only for part of the week.'

David cast her a curious glance, realising belatedly that she'd said something similar before. 'Then you've bought the cottage to use at weekends?'

'When I'm not on call, like this weekend. I wish I could make it my full-time home but it just isn't possible. I need to be close to the hospital during the week.' She must have sensed his interest because she explained. 'I'm a paediatric consultant.'

'I see. It must be interesting work.'

'Oh, it is. I always wanted to work with children right from the start, and I've never regretted it.' She cast him a quick smile. 'In fact, the reason I found my way to Yewdale was through one of the children I've been treating—Chloe Jackson. Do you know her?'

'Yes, of course. Emily was only saying earlier that Chloe had been into school today so I take it that she's on the mend? My partners have had more to do with the case than I have,' David added by way of explanation.

'Elizabeth and James?' Laura laughed as she saw his surprise. 'I met them when they came to visit Chloe who, I'm pleased to say, is responding very well to her treatment. We're really hopeful that she'll make a full recovery. But do tell me, have they worked things out yet?'

David frowned. 'Sorry...?'

Laura laughed as she changed gear, waiting until the throaty roar of the engine had settled down into a smooth hum once more before she continued. 'James and Elizabeth, I mean. It was obvious that they were crazy about each other when I met them, and equally obvious that neither of them had quite realised the fact. Did they work it out in the end?'

'Was it obvious?' David couldn't contain his surprise. 'I had no idea—' He broke off in sudden embarrassment, realising that he should have seen what had been happening right under his nose. The trouble was that he'd been so wrapped up in his own affairs since Kate had first been taken ill that a lot seemed to have passed him by. It made him uncomfortable to have to admit it so his tone was flat when he replied to the question.

'Elizabeth and James are engaged to be married so I think we can safely assume that they've worked things out.'

'Good! There's nothing like a happy ending, is there?' Laura grinned at him, then sobered abruptly as she obviously caught some fleeting expression on his face. 'Emily told me about her mother. I'm very sorry. It must have been hard for all of you.'

Her sympathy was completely genuine and David couldn't deny the surprise he felt on realising it. He'd come to resent the trite expressions of sorrow in the months after Kate died, but there had been nothing trite about those quietly spoken words. But, then, he sensed that Laura Mackenzie would never say anything she didn't mean. The thought shook him a little even though he wasn't sure why it should.

'Thank you. It *was* extremely hard, especially for the children. Emily seems to have got over it best of all. Mike has had problems, though, mainly with his schoolwork, but I think he's coming to terms with what happened at last. But as for Holly…' David sighed, feeling the pang he always felt when he thought about his oldest daughter.

'Emily told me that her sister had gone away. Was it because of your wife dying? Was that Holly's way of coping with it?'

'How did you…?' David began, stunned by her perception.

'Know?' Laura sighed. 'Because people deal with a bereavement in many different ways, but everyone goes through the same emotions eventually—sorrow, guilt, anger at the loved one for dying… I've seen it all too often in the course of my work, unfortunately. I imagine Holly will come to terms with what has happened in her own time. Going off like this is just her way of getting through it.'

'I expect you're right. Holly was at medical school when Kate died, and it seemed to hit her even harder because there was nothing anyone could do about it. She told me that she didn't see any point in carrying on with her studies and took off. She sends me postcards and phones occasionally. The last I heard she was in Brazil.'

'Then she hasn't cut herself off completely. She'll come back eventually when she's got everything straight in her own mind.' Laura smiled gently. 'You watch, Holly will turn up at your door one night.'

'I hope so,' David replied fervently, wondering why it felt as though a weight had been lifted off his shoulders all of a sudden. He'd tormented himself with the thought that he should have been able to help his daughter through this difficult period, but maybe Holly did need to work it out for herself. That it was Laura who'd made him see that came as a surprise. How could this stranger understand that when he hadn't been able to?

The thought was more than a little disturbing so he quickly steered the conversation away from himself. 'So, what about you, Laura? Have you a husband and a family?'

'Nope.' Laura reached back over the seat and patted the dog. 'No husband, no children, just Peebody.'

'Really?' David heard the surprise in his voice and knew that Laura had also caught it because she shot him a laughing glance.

'That doesn't mean that I wouldn't want both of those things,' she explained, 'although one would need to be the direct result of the other. I tend to be rather old-fashioned in some respects. I'd prefer to have a husband before the children arrived!'

David laughed at the wryness in her voice 'A very old-fashioned view these days! I can't believe there haven't been offers, though.'

'Not as many as you might think. Working the kind of hours I do, there isn't a lot of time left over for socialising. That's what ended my last relationship— he couldn't accept that my work played such a major role in my life.'

There was a steely note in her soft voice and a determined set to her beautiful mouth that told David she wasn't a woman who would allow herself to be pushed around. He felt a growing admiration for her, which he firmly squashed. Allow his emotions just a little leeway around Laura Mackenzie and there was no knowing what would happen

He turned to stare through the windscreen as they reached a bend in the road, realising how unsettled it made him feel to admit that. Maybe it would help to confine her to the role she was playing at present—that of the helpful neighbour. If he could mentally slot her into that nice tidy category then surely there wouldn't be a problem.

They hit the bend and David had to grab hold of the doorhandle as he felt himself sliding across the bench seat. He straightened abruptly but not before he'd got a whiff of some pungent aroma coming off Laura. It was nothing like the perfume he'd noticed her wearing earlier, but it was strangely familiar...

His mind clicked as it made the quantum leap towards recognition, although it was hard to believe the answer it came up with. Turpentine?

David stared fixedly through the windscreen as his heart began to pound erratically. How on earth could he slot a woman who doused herself in turpentine as readily as Chanel No. 5 into any sort of category?

'There...can you see the lights?' David pointed to a spot halfway up the steep hill and Laura nodded.

'Yep, got it!' She worked down through the gears with smooth efficiency, before setting the Land Rover at the incline. Gary Morrison must have heard them coming because he had the door open before they'd stopped, and came racing out to meet them.

'Thank God. You've got here, Dr Ross. I didn't know what to do...'

'How's Anna? Can you see the baby's head yet?' David cut short the younger man's hysteria as he climbed out of the car. He glanced round as Laura came to join him, quickly making the introductions. 'This is my new neighbour, Dr Laura Mackenzie. She kindly offered me a lift when my car wouldn't start.'

'Pleased to meet you.' Gary started back to the house at a run, speaking over his shoulder. 'Anna's very scared, Dr Ross. We both are. I can see the top of the baby's head all right, but nothing seems to be happening.'

He led the way into the sitting-room where Anna Morrison was lying on a makeshift bed of blankets and towels. Before David could put his case down Laura went straight over and crouched beside the young woman.

'Hello, Anna. I'm Laura Mackenzie. I've moved into the house next door to Dr Ross. I'm a doctor, too, so I thought I would come along and help out. How far apart are your contractions?'

'Every three…four minutes, I think, but I'm not sure…' Anna's face was covered in perspiration, her eyes full of fear. 'I'm so scared that something is going to go wrong and the baby will die!'

'Don't be.' Laura put her hand on the girl's distended abdomen and smiled encouragingly. 'I can feel your baby moving around. All he or she needs is a bit of help to get out of there. Now, you just try to relax. I'm going to talk you through this. OK?'

David could barely hide his surprise as he saw Anna smile. There was no doubt that Laura's presence had had an immediate calming effect. He crouched beside the two women, glancing curiously at Laura as he began to examine Anna. 'Have you delivered many babies?'

Laura grinned. 'Dozens! But that was several years ago when I did a stint with the UN out in Africa.' She gave Anna another encouraging smile. 'Mind you, it does mean that I'm used to working under all sorts of conditions. Most of the babies I delivered were born out in the bush where there were few medical facilities so this should be a doddle compared to that!'

David laughed. 'Seems to me that you couldn't have planned this better, Anna. Two doctors for the price of a phone call, and one of them who obviously prefers to spurn the comforts of a hospital delivery suite!'

Anna managed a weak smile. 'Maybe it's a good omen, then?'

'Of course it is—' Laura broke off as the girl gasped when another contraction began. 'Now, I want you to breathe slowly. Just try to relax and let your body do the job it's made to do. Don't fight the pain, Anna. Work with it instead.'

David could see the improvement immediately as Anna's tense muscles began to relax. He checked on the position of the baby's head, seeing immediately that it was pressing hard against the perineal tissues. Although it wasn't at full term, he guessed that the baby was fairly large and having difficulty in making its way into the world.

He got up and drew Gary aside, aware that Laura was still speaking to Anna in that same soothing tone, which was so effective. He was suddenly glad that she was there. Laura possessed the rare gift of being able to put people at ease, he realised—not for the first time that night.

'How long ago did Anna's waters break, Gary? Do you remember?'

'A few minutes before I spoke to you on the phone.' Gary cast an anxious glance at his wife. 'She is going to be all right, isn't she, Dr Ross? I feel so damned helpless!'

'Anna will be fine. The baby is fully viable at this stage and, from what I can tell, shouldn't be all that small either. Now it's simply a question of helping him or her out into the world.'

David clapped the worried father on the shoulder and went back to his patient. Laura was wiping Anna's face with a damp cloth. She glanced around as David knelt beside her, and he was struck once more by her beauty.

How many women could still look so good in a situation like this? he found himself wondering. And how many women would care so little about how she looked? he amended, noticing how every scrap of Laura's attention was focused on the other woman. All Laura was concerned about was the young mother and her baby. A layer of the ice which had encased David's heart for so long began to melt.

'The contractions are very close together now,' Laura informed him in a low voice. She glanced at Anna and automatically reached for the girl's hand as another contraction began. 'How are things progressing?'

'They're not. We seem to be at a bit of a standstill.' David lowered his voice so that Anna couldn't hear. 'The perineal tissues don't seem as though they're going to stretch any more so I'm going to do an episiotomy. I don't want any more pressure put on the baby's head, with it being premature.'

Laura nodded. 'That should help speed things up. I don't like the idea of this continuing too long. The baby could become distressed and we don't have the equipment to deal with it.'

'Exactly my sentiments.' David gave her a warm smile, pleased that she agreed with his decision. He glanced over to where Gary was pacing the floor, and quickly decided that it might be better if the young man wasn't in the room.

'Can you fetch me a bowl of hot water, please, Gary? But boil it first, will you?' he asked, suggesting

the first thing that came to mind. He saw Laura's brows
rise and then her quiet smile as she realised what he
was doing. She seemed to read his mind only too easily—

David cut short that disquieting thought, concentrating instead on explaining to Anna what he was going
to do and why. The girl barely seemed able to take it
in, nodding her agreement as he went to his case and
swiftly prepared an injection of local anaesthetic.
Within a few minutes the neat incision had been made
in the taut perineal tissues. With Laura talking Anna
through her breathing, David was free to concentrate
on delivering the child, gently supporting its head then
easing its tiny body free.

It was a little girl, small but not worryingly so.
However, it was not so much her size that concerned
David as the fact that she made no attempt to breathe.
He held the baby's head lower than her body to drain
any mucus from her nose and throat and tapped the
soles of her feet, but she still made no effort at all to
take a breath.

'What's the matter? Why isn't it crying?' Anna was
almost frantic as she tried to get up.

Laura pressed her back with a firm hand. 'No. Stay
there.'

Taking the baby from David, she laid it across her
knees then quickly bent and covered its nose and
mouth with her own mouth to blow air into its tiny
lungs. Anna was sobbing now, a heartbroken wail that
provided a background to the steady rhythm of Laura's
breathing as time and again she breathed into the
baby's lungs.

David had never felt more helpless as he watched
what was happening. He knew that he couldn't do any

more than Laura was doing, but it was no comfort to realise that. All he could do was pray for the child, and that seemed so little in the circumstances.

Laura raised her head and her blue eyes were full of pain as they met his before she bent back to the task.

The baby suddenly twitched, her arms and legs shooting out as she took her first breath. She gave a tiny mewing wail, opened her mouth and gave a decidedly lusty cry as she voiced her disapproval of the big wide world she found herself in.

'Yes!' Laura's face was filled with joy as the baby's cries rang around the room. With exquisite gentleness she swaddled the little girl in a towel and handed her tenderly to her sobbing mother. 'You have a beautiful little girl, Anna. Congratulations.'

'A girl…a daughter…' Anna sniffed back her tears, turning a wondering smile towards her husband as he came rushing into the room with an overflowing bowl of water. 'It's a girl, Gary—a little girl!'

'A girl? I don't know what to say…' There were tears in Gary's eyes as he knelt down and gently touched his daughter's crumpled little cheek.

David smiled. 'Your daughter seems to be saying everything that needs to be said!'

Everyone laughed as the baby gave another hearty wail. By the time the ambulance arrived a short time later everything had been sorted out—the baby bathed and dressed in a tiny white gown and bonnet and Anna tidied up for the journey. She would need to have the episiotomy repaired on arrival at the hospital as it was too delicate a task to be undertaken with such limited facilities. However, David was certain there wouldn't be any problems once the cut had healed.

The baby was put straight into the incubator that the

paramedics had brought with them. She'd need moni-
toring for the first forty-eight hours, but she seemed
remarkably healthy considering her summary arrival in
the world. Gary Morrison pumped David's hand and
kissed Laura on the cheek.

'Thank you, Dr Ross. And you, too, Laura. Neither
Anna nor I will ever forget what you both did tonight.'

Laura hugged him. 'I'm just so pleased for you both.
Maybe I can pop round to see Anna and the baby when
they get home from hospital?'

'You do that! You'll be very welcome.' Gary gave
them a last broad smile before he went to join his wife
and daughter. The ambulance roared away into the
night, leaving behind a feeling of anticlimax after all
the excitement.

David turned to Laura to thank her for all her help
and suddenly realised she was crying. 'What is it?'

'Nothing.' She gave a shaky laugh as she ran her
hand over her eyes. 'Just me being silly, that's all.'

She made a valiant attempt to smile but it was
spoiled as tears flooded her eyes once more. David
wasn't even aware of what he was doing as he drew
her into his arms. All he knew was that he hated to see
her crying like this.

'Shh. The baby will be fine,' he soothed, feeling her
small body trembling as she tried to hold back the sobs.

'Yes. I know she will. It's just so silly, really, but I
was so afraid...' Laura bit back another sob, nestling
her face into his shoulder so that he couldn't see her
tears.

David felt a wave of tenderness wash over him as
he gently turned her face up to his gaze. 'I know how
scary it was but it's all over now. Anna and Gary have
a beautiful little girl, thanks to you.'

Laura shook her head. 'No, it was you, David. The baby might not have made it if you hadn't acted so quickly by giving Anna that episiotomy.'

'But you were the one who resuscitated her...' he began, then laughed wryly. 'All right, let's just agree that we both played a vital part in it, shall we?'

'Agreed!'

Laura laughed softly as she stared up at him with luminously blue eyes. David knew to the very second when his desire to comfort her turned into another sort of desire entirely. He felt his head swim as he was assailed by a flood of emotions all at once—a burning need to kiss those beautiful lips that were smiling at him, an overwhelming urge to feel that deliciously feminine body pressed against his own, an almost unbearable yearning to find in Laura Mackenzie everything he'd lost...

He let her go so fast that she gasped. He knew he should say something but the words seemed to be locked in some pain-filled place deep inside him. It was left to Laura to break the silence, which she did in a flat little monotone.

'We'd better get back. The children will be wondering where you are.'

She turned and walked back to the car without another word. David watched as she opened the door and leaned inside to pat the dog. Her face was lit by the glow from the interior light, her delicate profile outlined against the darkened backdrop of mountains.

He closed his eyes, not wanting to see anything more, not needing any reminders of what he'd felt as he'd held Laura in his arms. He was going to have the devil's own job living with himself as it was!

CHAPTER THREE

A GUILTY conscience proved to be an uncomfortable bedfellow so that David spent a restless night. He got up a little before six the next morning and went downstairs, moving quietly so as not to wake Mike and Emily as he made his way to the kitchen and plugged in the kettle. He opened the kitchen door and stood looking out across the garden while he waited for the water to boil, trying to rid his mind of the myriad thoughts that had plagued him throughout the night.

Nothing had happened! he told himself for the umpteenth time, but it still didn't lessen the sense of guilt he felt. He'd wanted Laura last night—wanted to hold her and kiss her, to lose himself in her sweetness—and knowing that almost tore him in two.

The kettle came to the boil and David sighed as he went to make himself a mug of instant coffee. He spooned granules into the mug then went to the fridge for some milk, pausing as he spotted the picture affixed to its door with four colourful magnets.

He smiled, realising it was the picture Emily had been drawing the night before—he recognised that lime-green grass with no difficulty! However, it was a moment before he realised what the rest of it portrayed, and seemed to feel his heart land with a thump at his feet.

Emily had drawn their house, with them standing in front of it, but she'd added someone else to the line-up. David wished he could convince himself that he was mistaken, but there was little doubt in his mind that the figure with yellow hair was meant to be Laura! Emily had even drawn her dog, Peebody, in the background.

David stared at the picture with anguished eyes. It was a typical child's drawing of a family, the only trouble being that Laura shouldn't have featured in it at all. Did Emily see Laura as a…a substitute for her mother? Was that what this picture was all about? In view of what had happened, that idea was going to cause him a few more sleepless nights.

Saturday mornings in the surgery were usually quiet. They dealt only with urgent cases then so it needed only one of them to attend to any patients who arrived. David was glad it was his turn to provide cover that day. At least while he was concentrating on his work he had less time to brood.

He buzzed through to Reception to let Eileen know he was ready for his first patient, and smiled when Fred Murray walked into the room. A widower in his late sixties, Fred owned Boundary Farm which lay to the east of the town. His son, Peter, who lived with him, did most of the heavy work now that Fred was semi-retired

David greeted him with a smile, 'Good morning, Fred. Sit down and tell me what I can do for you.'

'Dr Ross.' Fred sat himself down in the chair and glanced around the room. He appeared a little nervous so David immediately tried to put him at ease.

'So, how's things at the farm? Did you have a good lambing season?'

'Aye, can't grumble. We lost a couple of young 'uns, but that's to be expected. Weather's been in our favour so that helped. Can't remember when we had such a mild spring,' Fred replied, although he still looked tense.

'The weather must make a big difference in your line of work—it does in mine, too, funnily enough,' David said encouragingly. 'We've not had half so many coughs and colds this year as we usually do.'

'Imagine that's right.' Fred cleared his throat. 'Well, it's not a cough or a cold I've come about this morning, Dr Ross. I've been having a bit of trouble, you see, with the old waterworks.'

David made a rapid translation, well used to the oblique way in which some people explained their problems. 'You're having trouble passing urine, are you, Fred? How long has it been going on for?'

'Oh, some while now—a year, maybe more.' Fred shifted uncomfortably. He was obviously well aware that he should have visited the surgery sooner so David didn't waste time, pointing it out.

'Just tell me what sort of symptoms you've been experiencing, Fred. It will help me determine what needs to be done,' he advised patiently.

'Well, at first it was just a case of it being hard to pass anything. Now, though, I seem to be always running back and forth to the toilet all the time.' Fred looked down at his gnarled hands. 'Gets a bit embarrassing, you understand, Doctor. I'm getting a bit of stick off the lads so I thought maybe I'd best come along and have a word with you to see if owt can be done.'

'It sounds to me as though your prostate gland is enlarged, Fred. It's fairly common in men over fifty, and it usually causes symptoms just like those you described—difficulty in passing urine to begin with, then a growing frequency in urination as the bladder becomes over-active to compensate for the obstruction. I'll need to examine you so if you'd like to pop behind the screen I'll take a look and see if I'm right.'

When Fred was ready David carefully made his examination, and soon discovered that his suspicions were correct. The prostate gland was far larger than it should have been. After telling Fred to get dressed again, he went back to his desk and waited for the man to join him.

'I'm ninety-nine per cent certain that it's an enlarged prostate, causing the trouble, Fred. And because it's got to this stage I'm afraid it's going to need operating on.'

'I did wonder...' Fred sighed. 'So, what happens now, Dr Ross?'

'I'll get in touch with the hospital and arrange for you to be seen by a consultant. He'll want you to have an ultrasound scan to see how big the prostate gland is, and probably blood and urine tests to see if the kidneys have been affected in any way, although, hopefully, that won't have happened. After that it's a case of removing the prostate as soon as possible,' David explained.

'And that will be the end of it?' Fred asked.

'Hopefully, yes. Why do you ask?'

'Iris—that's our Peter's wife—was reading this here article in one of those magazines she gets, and it said something about prostate trouble.' Fred stared at his feet, studiously avoiding David's eyes. 'She read it out to me as I can't see to read as well as I used. It mentioned something about cancer, Dr Ross.'

David sighed inwardly. He hadn't seen any point in worrying Fred unnecessarily, but now that Fred had raised the subject he had to tell him all the facts. 'There is a chance that the obstruction has been caused by a tumour forming in or around the prostate gland.'

'A tumour? By that you mean cancer, don't you? So that article was right, then?' Fred sounded worried and David hurried to reassure him.

'It's just a possibility, Fred. The prostate can enlarge without there being any sign of a malignant growth. The ultrasound scan will give the consultant a better idea what he's dealing with, though. If he's at all concerned, a biopsy will be done to verify if it is cancer. However, even if that turns out to be the case, the treatment is still the same and entails removing the prostate.'

David hoped he'd managed to reassure Fred Murray but he understood what a shock it had been for him. 'Try not to worry too much, Fred. I'll get onto the hospital right away so you should hear from them within the week.'

'Well, better to get it over and done with, I s'pose.' Fred sighed as he put his cap back on. 'If it i'n't one thing it's another. Our Peter and Iris have had enough to put up with lately, what with young Billy getting himself into such a mess. Expect you heard about that, didn't you, Dr Ross?'

David nodded. Not much escaped the local grapevine and news that Fred's grandson, Billy, was the father of the baby Sophie Jackson was expecting had soon got round the town. 'I heard.'

Fred laughed wryly. 'Thought so! Still, it won't be the first babe that's born wrong side of the blanket nor the last! Mind, you try telling our Peter that. He's not been fit to live with since he found out!'

David laughed softly as the old man left. He could imagine the ructions going on at Boundary Farm. Billy was only seventeen, a year older than Sophie, so David doubted that either family was happy about what had happened.

David saw the rest of the patients, then sent Eileen home and locked up. The surgery was built onto the side of Yewdale House, where Elizabeth and her father lived. David found himself wondering if she and James would live in the house when they married. It would make sense, but maybe they preferred to find a place of their own to begin their married life? Sometimes you had to move on and make a fresh start—

He cut off that thought abruptly, afraid of where it might lead. He wasn't looking for a fresh start. He was happy with what he had, his work and the children...

Oh, yes? that tormenting little voice demanded. So happy that he'd felt like a spare part these past few months, as though there was no purpose to his life any more?

David tried to put that thought to the back of his mind as he made his way home, but it was hard to block it out. It didn't help that he had to walk because of his car being out of action. He'd wanted to make a start on mowing the lawn that day so the added delay, combined with the unsettling thoughts, didn't put him in the best of moods.

He pushed open the gate with uncharacteristic impatience and strode up the path, only to come to an abrupt halt as he heard Mike shouting frantically from the back garden, 'Look out, Emily! He's going to get you. Oh, no!'

David's heart was in his throat as he raced around the house so it was a second or two before he took in the scene that met him. Emily was sprawled on the grass, laughing her head off. She was soaked to the skin, her yellow T-shirt plastered to her. Peebody was standing beside her, happily shaking himself and sending showers of water in all directions. Mike was doubled up with laughter as he watched, and Laura had both hands over her mouth, trying to contain her mirth.

David felt his temper erupt at the fright he'd had, thinking that something awful had happened to Emily, combined with everything else that had gone on in the past twelve hours.

'What the hell is going on here?' he demanded as he strode across the grass.

Mike and Emily swung round in surprise at the sound of his angry voice, but he barely glanced at them. His gaze was focused on the woman standing a little way off, her blonde hair curling damply around her face. She was soaking wet as well, David noticed, her bright blue shorts clinging to her bare thighs and her white blouse sporting huge damp patches all down the front.

David felt his body kick into action, felt the surge of heat hit him so hard that he almost stopped as he took in Laura's enticingly dishevelled appearance. It was only the blazing anger he felt that kept him moving towards her.

'Just what is going on?' he repeated furiously as he came to a stop in front of her.

Laura's smile faded as she raised her head and stared him straight in the eyes. 'We were giving Peebody a bath. Unfortunately, he decided he'd had enough.'

'"We"? Do I take that to mean that Mike and Emily were helping you?' David could hear the harshness in his voice and on one level was shocked by it, yet the anger he felt—at himself, at her—drove him on.

'Yes. Why? Have you a problem with that?' Laura's

tone was suddenly icy. It sent a shiver of warning through him but he was beyond taking any notice.

'Yes, I have a problem with it,' he snapped back. 'A couple of problems, in fact. Number one is that Mike is supposed to be writing an essay, not helping you bath that dog. And as for Emily, I'd prefer it if you consulted me first before you involved my daughter in your plans. Understand?'

'Perfectly!' Laura gave him a smile that would have stopped a charging elephant in its tracks. 'But a word of advice, David—don't take it out on the children because you feel guilty!'

She started to walk away but David was so incensed that he caught her arm. 'What are you talking about? And what gives you the right to give advice about something you know nothing about?' he said angrily.

'You did!' Laura's eyes blazed at him, although David noticed that she lowered her voice so that it wouldn't carry to where Mike and Emily were standing. This was meant only for his ears, he realised, and felt his stomach lurch in anticipation at what she was going to say.

'It was *me* in your arms last night, David. Do you imagine that I didn't know what you were feeling then?' She took a quick breath and he felt the fight suddenly drain out of her. There was now a trace of uncertainty in her eyes as they clung to his. 'Do you think that I didn't feel the same things? The only difference is that I don't feel guilty about it and you do.'

She shrugged his hand off, calling to the dog as she slipped through the gap in the hedge. David felt his head swim as the shock hit him. Laura had felt it, too—that hunger, that need…?

'How could you, Dad?'

Mike's angry voice brought him back to the present. David turned round, but his son didn't give him a chance to speak.

'How could you speak to Laura like that? She didn't do anything wrong!'

'That's debatable.' David struggled to keep his tone even. 'You told me yourself that you had an essay to write and it was going to take all weekend. And just look at Emily. She's soaked to the skin.'

'She was only having a bit of fun—we both were. But maybe that isn't permitted in this house any more!'

Mike stormed back to the house, followed by a dejected-looking Emily. David sighed, knowing that it was his fault the situation had deteriorated to this point. Why on earth hadn't he kept a check on his temper, instead of jumping in at the deep end like that? Just because he felt guilty about last night...

He felt a ripple run under his skin as he recalled what Laura had said about feeling everything he'd felt. Had she really meant it?

He turned to stare towards the house on the other side of the hedge, then turned abruptly and went to fetch the mower from the shed. He wouldn't allow himself to wonder about that!

By the time evening arrived, David was seriously considering ringing Sam O'Neill and offering to take over any calls that came in that night. Mike and Emily had stayed in their rooms for most of the day, and both of them had been subdued over tea. David knew he was in the doghouse for what had happened that afternoon, and both children were determined to let him know it.

When Emily's friend, Kelly, rang to ask if Emily could stay the night at her house, David agreed immediately. Anything that would cheer up his daughter and stop him from feeling such a heel!

He walked Emily over to Kelly's house, somewhat cheered when the child gave him a big hug before she went inside. It seemed that Emily had forgiven him so maybe he should try to make his peace with Mike, he thought as he walked back home.

It proved a bit more difficult because Mike was at that age when parents were always in the wrong, and in this case David knew that he most certainly *had* been wrong. However, they finally ironed things out and Mike, taking full advantage of the fragile harmony, took himself off to his friend's house to listen to music rather than getting on with the infamous essay.

David sighed as the door slammed behind his son. He was beginning to feel like a fool for the way he'd behaved, but at least things were sorted out now... Or almost, he amended. There was one more person who deserved an apology, although he had a feeling that it would be the most difficult one to make.

Peebody set up a tremendous racket when he knocked on Laura's door a few minutes later. David leaned against the wall, mentally rehearsing what he would say. All it needed was a few brief words to explain how much he regretted his outburst...

He experienced a momentary qualm as he wondered if Laura would make any mention of the previous night again. How would he explain that away?

'Hello, David.'

He felt his stomach roll over as he heard her voice. He swung round, trying his hardest to ignore the way his heart began to pound as he saw her standing by the side of the house. She was still wearing the shorts she'd had on earlier and her slender legs and feet were bare.

However, she'd exchanged the blouse for an old T-shirt in a washed-out shade of blue, which simply made her eyes look even bluer in contrast. She was holding a wine glass in her hand, and as he watched she lifted it to her lips and took a sip of the rose-pink wine…

David's hands clenched and he had to look away as her throat moved convulsively when she swallowed. He couldn't believe the urge he felt to reach out and let his fingers run down the delicate column of her neck. The effort to control how he was feeling was so great that his voice rasped when he spoke, making the words sound unnaturally harsh in the quiet of the evening.

'I wonder if I might have a word? It won't take long.'

'Of course. I was in the back garden. Come on through.' She turned and made her way back round the house, leaving David with little choice but to follow her. He sighed as he made his way along the path. He'd been hoping to make his apology then leave, but it seemed it might take a little longer than he'd expected.

Laura was sitting on the grass under the apple tree when he reached the back garden. An old grey blanket spread on the ground bore the remains of a meal. David came to a halt as he saw the exquisite china and silverware, and suddenly realised that the glass she'd been drinking from was Waterford crystal. His eyes flew to Laura's blue ones in open astonishment, and he heard her laugh.

'I don't mind pigging it but I do like to do it in style!' She took the bottle of wine out of the silver ice bucket and held it out for his inspection, her smile widening as she saw him blink. 'I also like good wine on the rare occasions I indulge. Can I tempt you—to a glass of wine, I mean?'

David felt his stomach perform that extraordinary manoeuvre again, a sort of spiralling somersault that left him feeling all shaken up as he heard the laughter in her voice. He could scarcely believe his ears, but Laura was definitely teasing him about how he'd felt last night… About how they'd both felt! he amended incredulously.

'I… Yes. Thank you,' he responded, praying that his voice didn't betray the shock he felt. He wasn't used to people being so open about their feelings that it threw him off balance, and he wasn't sure how to react.

'Good. I'll just fetch another glass. But give me a couple of minutes to find one. I haven't unpacked more than the basics, which boils down to one of everything. I wasn't expecting visitors so don't run away. We may as well make our apologies over a glass of wine, and enjoy the occasion.'

The lilting sound of her laughter carried back across the garden as she made her way towards the house. David sat down a shade abruptly on the blanket, feeling as though he was suddenly out of his depth.

How had Laura known that he'd come to apologise? he wondered, then sighed ruefully. Wasn't it obvious? Both of them knew he'd gone over the top this afternoon. The thought did nothing to set his mind at rest.

'Right, that didn't take as long as I thought it might.' Laura came back with a glass. She filled it with wine then handed it to him, making no attempt to avoid contact as their fingers brushed. David felt a shiver dance through his fingertips, and knew at once that Laura had felt the very same thing.

The realisation both stunned and shocked him. He'd

met this woman barely twenty-four hours before so how *could* he know so much about her?

'A toast,' Laura raised her glass. 'To apologies, both given and accepted. Will you drink to that, David?'

It was such a graceful way of smoothing out the events of that day that David raised his glass as he repeated the toast in a low voice. Laura made things so easy and yet so complicated. He'd never met anyone who was such a bundle of contradictions.

He took a sip of wine, wondering if he would ever understand her. He caught himself up short. Why did he need to understand her? Laura was his neighbour, no more or less than that, he reminded himself sternly, then tried to close his mind to the mocking internal laughter that greeted that thought

Laura might be a lot of things, but it would be wishful thinking on his part to try to put her into any sort of category.

'Have you eaten? There's some chicken left, if you want it...' she began.

David shook his head, pleased that he could latch onto such a safe topic of conversation. 'No, I've already eaten, thanks. But don't let me spoil your dinner.'

'Oh, you're not! I'm absolutely stuffed to the gills, to tell the truth. That's the trouble with cooking for one—you end up making far too much. Still, it'll keep till tomorrow and what I don't finish Peebody will. That animal is a veritable four-legged dustbin!'

'It must cost a fortune, feeding him.' David laughed, feeling more at ease. He leaned back on his elbow and picked up a piece of apple blossom which had dropped onto the blanket, smoothing the velvety petals between his fingers.

'It does. I imagine that's why his previous owners got rid of him.' Her smile faded as she glanced over to where the dog lay sprawled on the grass.

'I found him wandering the streets a year or so back. He was little more than a bag of bones, starving and terrified. He'd obviously been ill treated because if you made any sudden move—raised your hand or jumped up too quickly—he cowered. He wasn't house-trained either, hence the name! I kept him when nobody came forward to claim him.'

'He was lucky you found him, Laura,' David said quietly.

'Thank you.' She accepted the compliment calmly and David felt a little start of surprise at her lack of artifice. Laura didn't play the sort of games most people played. Because she spoke the truth she expected others to do the same. It was more than a little disquieting in view of earlier revelations.

'How do you manage when you're at work? He's a big dog so I imagine he needs a lot of exercise,' he asked quickly, to cover the confusion he felt.

'Oh, Peebody is very accommodating. If you want to take him for a five-mile run, he'll happily go with you. But if you can only squeeze in a quick ten minutes, he's just as happy to fall in line. Fortunately, my flat has a garden so a neighbour lets him out several times a day.' Laura raised her glass to her lips, sighing in contentment. 'Mmm, this is pleasant. It's so peaceful here. I wish I'd decided to buy myself a place in the country sooner, although at times over these past couple of weeks I have wondered if I was mad!'

David's brows rose. 'Why is that?'

'Because I decided to do all the work on the house myself.' She grimaced but there was laughter in her eyes. 'I didn't realise just what I was letting myself in for!'

David found himself laughing with her. There was something irresistible about her warmth and spontaneity. 'Bitten off more than you can chew?' he teased.

'Too right!' She jumped to her feet suddenly and held out her hand. 'Come on, let me show you what I've done so far. I haven't had anyone to show it off to as yet, and I'm rather proud of my efforts!'

David automatically took her hand and let her pull him to his feet, trying to ignore the sudden lurch his heart gave as he found himself standing so close to her that it would have been impossible to slip a sheet of paper between them. Laura's smile faded slowly, her blue eyes reflecting a wealth of emotions that made David's heart race. Suddenly, the air around them seemed to be charged with energy, as though an electric current were arcing between them.

'David…'

His name was tender as it slid from her lips, the wistfulness of her tone making David feel as though he were going to explode. Heat was building inside him, infusing every cell in his body with warmth. He was barely aware of raising his hand so the feel of her cool skin beneath his fingertips came as a shock.

It felt so soft, he thought wonderingly. As soft and delicate as the blossom he'd touched just a few moments before. What would her lips feel like? Cool and soft, like those flower petals, or warm?

Her eyes held his fast as he bent towards her, the awareness in them making his heart race even more. Laura knew he was going to kiss her and was making no attempt to stop it from happening because it was what she wanted as much as he did—

'Hello! Are you there, David?'

David felt as though the ground had dropped away beneath him as he heard someone shouting his name. He swung round in time to see Sam O'Neill appear round the side of the house. For a moment they all stayed right where they were—his hand still cupping Laura's face, their bodies just touching—and then Sam gave a faintly embarrassed laugh.

'Sorry, I hope I'm not interrupting anything!'

CHAPTER FOUR

'WELL, thanks for these, David. Do you want me to drop them off on my way back or what?' Sam O'Neill jangled the bunch of keys David had just given him. David shook his head. He was trying his hardest to handle this with an outward calm but it wasn't easy.

'No, there's no need to bother. You can give them back to me on Monday,' he instructed tersely, then groaned inwardly as he saw the knowing smile Sam gave him. Did Sam imagine that he didn't want him coming back because he'd be in the way? David had the uncomfortable feeling that he did!

'Fine. I'm only glad that I managed to track you down. What with Liz and James being away, I'd have been stuck otherwise. Of all the stupid things to do, leaving my surgery keys in my desk drawer!' Sam grimaced and Laura laughed at his wry expression.

'It's easily done, especially when you have a lot on your mind. I've locked myself out so many times that I leave a spare set of keys to my flat with a neighbour! I've had to use them twice in the past couple of weeks, in fact.'

Sam's brows rose. 'Oh, so you're not living here full time then?'

'Oh, no, I live in the city, for my sins. This is a little haven to escape to when the going gets too tough!' Laura laughed. If she was at all disconcerted by Sam's arrival it didn't show. David wished he could emulate her easy manner but, then, it *was* easier for her. Laura didn't have her conscience to answer to as he did, and at that moment his conscience was giving him a very hard time indeed!

'I'd better get back,' he said quickly, in what he hoped was an even tone. 'Mike will wonder where I am if he gets home and I'm not in.'

'Of course.' Laura's tone matched his yet David suspected that she knew he was just making an excuse to leave.

He avoided her eyes, not wanting to see the awareness in them. There was no point in lying to himself. If Sam hadn't turned up then he'd have kissed Laura, let himself enjoy the sweetness of her lips...

'I'll see you on Monday,' he said abruptly to Sam, closing his mind to what might have been. The self-contempt he felt should have made that easy to do, but he couldn't deny that just remembering how it had been to feel her softness pressed against him made his blood race. 'If you have any problems give me a ring. I'll be in all night.'

He turned to go but paused as Laura suddenly called out to him. His hands clenched at the sound of his name coming from her lips once more. Why did he respond like that just because she said his name in that soft voice? Why did he feel so churned-up inside? He couldn't understand it but he did understand the guilt that followed so swiftly in its wake. He knew only too well why he felt that!

'Yes?' His tone was curt as he turned, but Laura didn't appear disconcerted by it. David sensed she understood what he was going through, although that didn't make him feel any better.

He didn't want this woman to understand him. He didn't want there to be anything at all between them.

The only woman who'd had the right to know how
he'd felt had been Kate.

'I'll be leaving early in the morning. I need to get
back to see a patient who's being admitted tomorrow.
I only got to know about it this afternoon. Will you tell
Emily that I'll see her next week and that I haven't
forgotten my promise?'

'Promise?' David queried, and heard Laura laugh at
his evident surprise.

'Mmm, I meant to mention it before. In fact, it's the
reason I called round to see you last night. I promised
Emily that she could help me do some stencilling on
the kitchen walls, you see. However, bearing in mind
that I always seem to get myself covered in paint, I
thought I should warn you that Emily will need to wear
her very oldest clothes!'

'Perhaps it would have been better if you'd spoken
to me first, before suggesting it to Emily.' David could
hear the bite in his voice. Suddenly he felt angry. No
wonder Emily was getting fanciful notions in her head
and drawing pictures like the one taped to the fridge.

Laura had no right to involve his daughter in her life
like this. He hadn't realised to what extent it was happening, but now he could see how Emily might be
getting the wrong idea. Maybe Laura welcomed the
child's company when she knew few other people in
the town, but she had no idea of the repercussions it
could cause. The last thing he wanted was for Emily
to get hurt.

'In future, I'd prefer it if you consulted me before
making plans for my children. I thought I made that
clear this afternoon.'

'Oh, you did. Silly of me to imagine that you'd
changed your mind, Dr Ross, wasn't it?' Laura gave

him a smile which could have drawn blood. Her blue eyes were like shards of glass as they warred with his. 'I imagined that was why you came round tonight—to see that I understood the situation properly.'

She looked deliberately at the two glasses standing side by side on the old grey blanket, then gave a tinkly little laugh that grated on his raw nerves. 'Still, we seem to have everything clear now, don't we?'

She didn't give David a chance to say anything more as she turned to Sam. 'Right, come along, then. I am dying to show off what I've done in the house to someone so I'm not letting you escape until you've had the full guided tour. And don't stint on the compliments. I have a very high embarrassment threshold, believe me!'

'I'll bear that in mind!' Sam laughed but there was a touch of uncertainty in the look he shot at David before he followed Laura towards the house.

David swung round and made his way back through the hedge, telling himself that he didn't care what was going on next door. So what if Sam O'Neill was being shown around Laura's house? What business was it of his? The damned woman could invite a whole regiment—a whole army even—and it wasn't any of his concern. Yet he went straight to the window after he got in and stood there until he saw Sam's car driving off a short time later. That he felt relieved was something he would never admit to. Laura meant absolutely nothing to him.

'What's this I hear about you and a beautiful stranger, being seen cavorting around the countryside together? Come on, David, let's hear all the juicy details!'

Abbie Fraser, the local district nurse, put a cup of

coffee on the desk in front of him and folded her arms.
'Now now! You've lived here long enough to know
that you can't keep secrets in this town!'

'What secrets? What have we missed?' Elizabeth
came into the room at that moment and caught the tail
end of the conversation. She glanced back at James,
who'd followed her, and raised her brows. 'Seems
something has been going on around here, and we were
only away for a couple of days!'

David picked up the cup. The coffee was burning
hot and stung his tongue, but it gave him an excuse
not to answer. He sighed as he realised they were all
waiting for him to say something. 'I imagine you're
talking about my new neighbour, Laura Mackenzie.
My car broke down on Friday and she very kindly offered me a lift out to Rowbottom Farm. Anna went
into labour early,' he added, hoping that would provide
a diversion.

'Did everything go OK?' Elizabeth asked anx-
iously—on cue. David smiled, relieved that there
wasn't going to be an inquest. He'd gone over and over
the events of the weekend until his head had spun, but
he still couldn't understand why he'd behaved the way
he had.

'She's fine, and so is the baby—a little girl who, I
believe, is going to be called Emma,' he hurriedly explained, before his thoughts got sidetracked again.
'They're both in hospital but there shouldn't be any
problems. The baby had a bit of trouble breathing at
first, but Laura managed to sort that out.'

The name slid out before he could stop it and David
winced inwardly at the slip as he saw Elizabeth's brows
rise enquiringly.

'Oh, is she a doctor, then—?' She broke off with a

laugh. 'Did you say Laura Mackenzie. Not the same Laura Mackenzie who's Chloe's consultant, by any chance?'

'Yes, so I believe.' David picked up a sheaf of papers, suddenly anxious to put an end to the conversation. 'Have you seen this yet? It's the estimate for setting up the video link to the hospital. And we've had the go-ahead from the area health authority. If we can find the money we could be up and running by the end of next month.'

He handed over the papers, pleased when everyone started discussing the plans to install a sophisticated new computer system into the practice. It was an exciting venture because the new system would allow patients to speak to a consultant at the hospital about a range of problems, simply by coming into the surgery. However, David had to admit that it was an effort to summon up much enthusiasm when his head was full of so many other things.

'Looks good to me.' James handed the papers to Sam to read, then smiled teasingly at Elizabeth. 'How about you, Beth? Not having any more second thoughts about all this new technology?'

Elizabeth laughed softly. She'd been very against the idea to begin with, although David suspected that her feelings had been bound up with her growing attraction to James. James had been the one to suggest that they install the new system, and during those first difficult weeks after he'd arrived in Yewdale Elizabeth had been adamantly opposed to the idea.

What a difference a few weeks could make! David thought wryly. But, then, what a difference a few days could make, he amended reluctantly. It was hard to

believe that he'd met Laura only a couple of days ago
when he considered the turmoil she'd caused…

'David?'

He jumped as Abbie tapped him on the arm. A little
colour rose to his face as he caught the look that passed
between her and Sam. Had Sam mentioned what he'd
seen on Saturday night? David wondered with a sink-
ing heart. Maybe he should have a word with Sam…
And say what? That Sam was mistaken? That he hadn't
seen David standing there with Laura in his arms? Both
of them knew what had been going on!

'Sorry, Abbie. I was just wondering how soon we
can get patients booked in to use the new video link,
assuming we can work out the finance,' he replied
quickly, to hide his dismay. He had loved Kate and the
thought that other people might think he'd forgotten
her so soon was unbearably painful.

'Well, from what folk have said to me, there won't
be a shortage of volunteers! Most people I've spoken
to have been very enthusiastic about the idea. I keep
trying to explain that it won't be suitable for *every*
complaint, but they seem disappointed when I tell them
that!' Abbie laughed.

'Anyway, before I forget, Marie Rogerson stopped
me as I was coming out of church yesterday. She's
really worried about her Cyril. Evidently, he did as you
said and didn't eat a thing until Saturday night but then
he was very sick again. Marie said that he's insisting
on going back to work today, but I could tell she wasn't
happy about it. I thought I'd better mention it to you.'

'I'm glad you did. I'll try to drop in and see him
later in the week. If I know Cyril he'll just try to soldier
on, but he wasn't well when I saw him. I'd been hoping
that it might have been a touch of food poisoning that

was causing all the trouble, but it doesn't look like it.' David made a note on his pad to call on Cyril Rogerson, then looked up as the buzzer sounded. 'Sounds as though the first patients have arrived.'

Everyone started to leave the room—apart from Sam, who lingered behind until the others had gone. He took some keys out of his pocket and dropped them on David's desk. 'Thanks for these, David. Mine were in my desk drawer, as I thought.'

'That's OK.' David slid them into his pocket, glancing up as he realised the locum was still standing there. Sam had been with them over a year now, far longer than anyone had expected him to stay. He was due to leave them at the end of September to go overseas to work, and David knew that they'd all miss him.

Sam's cheerful nature and good looks had endeared him to everyone in the town, especially the single girls! There was no shortage of admirers of the dashing Dr O'Neill, as Abbie teasingly referred to him. David found himself wondering if Laura had been drawn by the younger man's easy charm before he cut short that unworthy thought!

'Something bothering you, Sam?' he asked instead.

'I just wanted to apologise for butting in last night. I had no idea…' Sam shrugged. 'Well, you know.'

David did—only too well! And it didn't make him feel any better. He brushed aside the apology with a few quick words, sighing as Sam left the room. When did life start getting so *complicated*?

He knew the answer, of course. Things had started to change on Friday night when a small blonde woman in dungarees and a check work shirt had walked into his house and his life. He had the feeling that nothing was going to be quite the same ever again!

*   *   *

'There are some calls for you, David. Here you are.'
Eileen handed over the slips. Morning surgery had just
ended and it was his turn to go out to any house calls.
He checked through the list, pausing when he came to
one of the names.

'Did Annie Jackson say what was wrong with young
Sean?' he enquired, glancing at the ever-efficient
Eileen, who ran the surgery like clockwork.

'Just that he hadn't been feeling well and had a bit
of a temperature.' Eileen sighed. 'That poor woman
must be up to her eyes, what with little Chloe having
been so poorly and young Sophie expecting. I don't
know how she copes!'

'Neither do I. I think I'll go over there first. I believe
Chloe is home at the moment and I'm not happy about
her being in contact with anything possibly conta-
gious.'

David went outside and got into the car he'd hired
while his own car was off the road. It took only a few
minutes to drive the short distance to the Jacksons'
little terraced house, set in one of the side-streets off
the high street.

He parked behind a rusty old Ford Cortina which
reminded him suddenly of Laura's vehicle. Odd that
she should drive such a car, he thought before he could
stop himself. He sighed as he got out and went to ring
the bell. Laura was on his mind far too much, but trying
to do anything about it was proving harder than it
should have done!

Annie let him in and led the way upstairs to one of
the cramped bedrooms. 'Sean's been saying as he
hasn't felt well for a couple of days now, but I took
no notice.' She shook back her dyed blonde hair with
a sigh. 'He's not that keen on school so it isn't unusual,

you see, Dr Ross. But he did seem to be very hot this morning so I thought that maybe he wasn't trying it on and called you.'

'Well, let's take a look, shall we?' David went into the room, picking his way between the jumble of clothes and toys strewn across the floor. Annie's housekeeping left a lot to be desired, but it couldn't be easy to bring up five children on the little money coming into the house.

Her husband, Barry, did odd jobs around the town, supplementing their income with a bit of poaching when things got really tough! But five children were a lot to deal with, especially when one of them had been as ill as Chloe had been.

David turned his attention to Sean, seven years old and a real little rip. He sat down on the edge of the bunk bed, took a good look at the child and laughed. 'Well, I think I can safely say what's wrong with this young man—a classic case of mumps. Take a look.'

'Well, I never!' Annie sounded astounded as she saw the child's swollen cheeks. 'His face wasn't like that when I rang the surgery this morning.'

'I'm sure it wasn't. Sometimes the swelling can appear within a couple of hours. Has he been complaining of a sore neck, by any chance—maybe that it hurts to chew?'

'Why, yes he has! I took no notice to be honest, just thought it was something to do with his back teeth. Dentist said as they would start coming through soon. Mumps, though, well, I never!'

'Mumps isn't as common as it used to be,' David explained as he opened his case to find a thermometer to take Sean's temperature. 'Since the introduction of the MMR vaccine—measles, mumps and rubella, it stands for—there has been a huge decrease in the number of cases each year. Did Sean not have the vaccination, Annie?'

'I'm not sure…' Annie frowned. 'To tell the truth, it's hard to keep track, what with five of them. I think our Darren had it, and Stephen, but I don't know about the others… Oh! What about Chloe, Dr Ross? Could she catch it, too? They warned us at the hospital to be very careful, and now our Sean has to come down with this!'

'It's something we need to take into consideration.' David frowned as he took the thermometer from Sean's mouth. 'Hmm, not too bad, young man. How do you feel?'

'Hot, and it hurts when I swallow.' Sean was starting to look quite perky now he realised there might be a plus side to being ill. 'I won't have to go to school, will I, 'cos the others could catch it as well?'

'No, you can't go to school, although I know how disappointed you'll be about that!' David laughed as he ruffled Sean's spiky brown hair. He got up as the boy grinned happily, looking like a little hamster with his swollen cheeks. 'No school for at least a fortnight as there's always the chance that another child might not have been vaccinated and could catch it from you.

'In the meantime, Annie, keep him in bed for a day or so and make sure he has plenty to drink. I'll give you a prescription for a mild analgesic to relieve the discomfort, but there isn't much else we can do apart from that. As for Chloe, I suggest you keep her well away from her brother. I'll get on to the hospital and see what they advise.'

'Thank you, Dr Ross.' Annie led the way back downstairs and paused in the hall. 'How about Sophie?

You know she's expecting, I suppose. Is there any risk to the baby?'

'No. However, I think it's only sensible to keep her away from Sean as well as there's no point in her being ill. How is she doing, by the way? Has she decided what she's going to do about school?'

'They've been ever so good, Dr Ross. The headmaster told Sophie that she can stay on for the rest of this term and take her exams. The baby's due in October so he's arranged for her to go to the community college after Christmas. They have a nursery and everything there so they can cater for girls like Sophie. Sophie says she still wants to take her A levels, you see,' Annie added in explanation.

'Good for her. I know it must have been a big shock for all of you, but Sophie will manage, I'm sure,' David said encouragingly.

'I hope so. I don't want her ending up like me—not that I'd swop my kids, Dr Ross, you understand, but I wish I'd taken more notice at school then maybe got myself a decent job.' Annie sighed as she opened the door. 'Still, these things happen, don't they? And you just have to get on with them.'

'You do, indeed, Annie. I'll give you a call once I've spoken to the hospital about Chloe and let you know what they advise.'

'It's Dr Mackenzie you need to talk to. Lovely woman she is…' Annie laughed as she gave him a knowing look. 'But, there, I don't need to tell *you* that!'

David didn't say anything, but went to the car. He started the engine with a little more vigour than was necessary. It seemed that the whole town had heard about him and Laura being seen together the other night! He hated to think what interpretation was being put on it.

That thought kept him company as he attended to the rest of the calls. It didn't put him in the best of moods for making the phone call to the paediatric unit at the hospital once he got back to the surgery. He asked for Laura Mackenzie, trying to get a grip on himself before he spoke to her. This was a purely professional call, he reminded himself sternly, but he couldn't deny the way his heartbeat quickened as he recognized her voice coming down the line.

'Laura Mackenzie speaking. Can I help you?'

'It's David Ross here, Dr Mackenzie.' The formal title was almost laughable in view of what had happened that weekend, but David was determined to keep her at a distance.

She must have realised that because her response was equally formal. 'Dr Ross. What can I do for you?'

'It's about Chloe Jackson,' David explained, wondering why it stung to hear her adopt that chilly tone so readily. 'I've just been to the Jacksons' house, and it turns out that one of her brothers has come down with mumps. In view of her treatment, I thought I should ring and ask your advice.'

'I'm glad you did!' Laura's voice lost its chill immediately. David felt a ripple run through him as he heard the warmth flowing back into those sweetly husky tones once more. He closed his eyes, striving to keep a grip on himself, but he knew that he wasn't making a very good job of it. He felt all twisted up inside as the memory of those moments in Laura's garden came rushing back. He might hate himself for his own weakness but it didn't alter how he'd felt!

'So what do you suggest?' he asked tersely, praying that Laura couldn't guess how confused he felt.

'Frankly, I don't think we should take any risks. Chloe was due to come into hospital next week for more tests, but it might be better if she came in straight away. We'll put her in a side-room to avoid any contact with the other children on the ward and keep an eye on her.'

'That sounds like the ideal solution. Do you want me to tell her parents or will you contact them?' David asked.

'I'll give Annie a call and make the arrangements.' Laura paused 'About Saturday, David. I just wanted to say that I never meant to step on your toes in any way. It never occurred to me that you might object to Emily being at my house.'

David sighed. 'I may have gone a little over the top. It's just that I don't want Emily getting hurt.'

'Hurt?'

He heard the puzzlement in Laura's voice and could have bitten off his tongue. The last thing he wanted was to have to explain, and yet what choice did he have now that he'd come this far? 'I don't know how to put this, but Emily misses her mother. I…I was worried in case she becomes too attached to you. You have your own life to lead and I'm sure you don't want to be bothered with someone else's child.'

'I see. You're worried in case Emily starts to see me as a substitute for her mother—is that it, David?'

'I suppose so,' he replied reluctantly, uncomfortable with the blunt question. He felt a little start of surprise when Laura suddenly laughed.

'And you could very well be right!'

'Why do you say that?' David felt his stomach sink. 'What has Emily been saying to you?'

'Oh, nothing much apart from—' She suddenly broke off and David heard voices in the background. She came back on the line. 'I have to go. We've got a bit of a crisis here. Sorry.'

She'd hung up before he could draw breath. David put the receiver back on its rest and stared across the room. Exactly what *had* Emily been saying?

CHAPTER FIVE

THE week seemed to pass with excruciating slowness despite the fact that they were so busy at the surgery. David was seething with impatience to know what Emily had been saying to Laura to cause her such amusement. Several times he thought about broaching the subject with his daughter, but each time he shied away from doing so. He didn't want to make an issue out of it. He simply wanted to know what had been going on!

He dropped Emily off at Brownies on Thursday evening then drove home. His car was back from the garage and working perfectly now that it had had the long-overdue service. David parked in the drive and turned to go inside the house, then paused as he heard a vehicle coming up the lane. As he watched, a van drove past the gate and turned in next door. He only caught a glimpse of the driver, but even from that brief look he knew it wasn't Laura. What was going on?

He hesitated, wondering if he should go round and check that everything was all right. It was only Thursday, after all, and he wouldn't have expected Laura to be back just yet. Suddenly he heard the familiar sound of Laura's laughter coming through the hedge.

'Adam, you idiot—stop it! Stop it!'

David turned sharply on his heel and went inside, trying to ignore the unreasoning annoyance he felt. So what if Laura had brought someone with her? What business was it of his? It was her house and she was free to entertain anyone she chose to.

He went to the dining-room, got out the bottle of whisky he kept in the sideboard for emergencies and poured himself a small measure. Cradling the glass in his hand, he went back to the sitting-room and stared out of the window. He could just make out the roof of the van from where he stood and not a lot else. Where was Laura? What was she doing? And who was this man she'd brought with her? Adam, she'd called him—and a damned silly name it was, too.

His eyes were suddenly drawn to the bedroom window as a light went on in the room and Laura suddenly appeared. She turned to speak to someone and a second figure appeared at the window. The man looped a casual arm across Laura's shoulders as he bent to peer out—

David turned away, not needing to see anything more. He could imagine only too easily what was going on next door!

'I thought I'd try to catch you in, Cyril. I just wanted to see how you were feeling.' David stepped inside the hall when Cyril Rogerson opened the door for him.

It was Friday evening and surgery had just finished. It had been a spur-of-the-moment decision to drop in on Cyril on his way home. Mike and Emily were spending the weekend with Kate's mother so there wasn't the usual rush to get back home. As he saw how drawn and gaunt Cyril looked, David was suddenly glad that he had decided to come.

'That's good of you, Dr Ross.' Cyril led the way into the parlour, where once again a fire was burning in the grate. 'Marie's out at her WI meeting—she'll be sorry she missed you. But at least I can get a chance to tell you how I feel without her hearing. She worries so, you see.'

'She's bound to. You don't look well, Cyril, I have to say. Are you managing to eat anything?' David put his case down and took the chair at the other side of the fire, unbuttoning his jacket as the room was so warm.

'I try, Dr Ross, but I can't seem to keep anything down.' Cyril sighed as he held out his hands towards the blaze. David noticed how they trembled and felt more concerned than ever. In the week since he'd seen him, Cyril had definitely deteriorated. It made him more certain than ever that this wasn't some mild stomach bug but something far more serious, although finding out what was the problem.

'I feel so tired all the time, too,' Cyril continued. 'I don't know how I've managed to keep going this past week at work. It's been a real effort, I can tell you.'

'I think this has gone on long enough. I'd like to arrange for you to have some blood tests done to see if they can throw any light on what's wrong with you. Can you call into the surgery tomorrow morning? Dr Sinclair is on duty but I'll let him know you're coming in.'

'Yes, if you think it might help, Dr Ross. I wish I knew what was wrong with me, though. I was fine until we went to visit our Sarah.' Cyril smiled, valiantly trying to make light of his problems. 'Maybe the Norwich air didn't agree with me.'

'Maybe.' David laughed, wishing it was that simple. 'I'll just take your blood pressure while I'm here. And I want you to promise me that you'll let me know if any other symptoms occur. If we could find some clue to what is behind this, we'd be able to deal with it. At the moment it's very much a process of elimination.'

David checked Cyril's blood pressure but found that once again it was normal. He drove home after leaving the Rogersons' house, still pondering on what the trouble might be. Sometimes it wasn't easy to diagnose an illness, and this seemed to be so in Cyril's case, although, hopefully, the blood tests would help point him in the right direction.

He turned into his drive, carefully avoiding glancing towards the house next door. He'd tried his best not to think about Laura and her house guest but it hadn't been easy. At odd times David had found his mind going back to what he'd witnessed the night before. There had been a familiarity about the way that man's arm had dropped around her shoulders which had spoken volumes!

Who was he? Was it the man with whom Laura had had a relationship not so long ago? Or someone new who'd come into her life only recently?

David sighed as he slid his key into the lock. What business was it of his, anyway? Laura didn't owe him any explanations. She was a grown woman and it was up to her what she did and with whom she did it.

The thought was less settling than it should have been so David strove to put it out of his mind as he went to the kitchen and opened the fridge. Bacon, eggs, tomatoes… There was enough to make himself a meal but suddenly he couldn't be bothered.

To hell with it, he thought. He would go to the Fleece and get something there. He couldn't spend the rest of his days sitting on his own in this house. Kate wouldn't have wanted him to do that. She'd been so full of life herself that she'd never have expected him to sit at home and mourn for the rest of his days!

The Fleece was packed when David arrived. He threaded his way through the crowd, pausing to have a word with various people who stopped him as he made his way to the bar. Being a GP in a town like Yewdale, it meant that everyone knew him. It could be a bit of a problem at times, especially when he was called upon to dispense medical advice in the middle of the high street.

However, being part of the community was an aspect of his work he enjoyed most. It was obviously something that appealed to Laura Mackenzie, he realised, as he spotted her sitting at the bar.

David hesitated, not wanting it to look as though he was going over to join her. However, at that moment she saw him and waved, leaving him little option but to go over. He was conscious of the interested glances being cast their way.

'Hi, David. Come and have a drink—it's my round!' she leaned across the bar, beckoning to Harry Shaw, the publican. 'Same again, please, Harry, plus whatever David is having.'

'Just a half of shandy, please, Harry. I'm on call tonight.' David took the stool beside her, glancing around at the rest of the group. Frank Shepherd was there with his wife, Jeannie, and Abbie and Sam, too. He smiled at them, trying not to take too much notice of the looks they exchanged.

Did they think that he'd arranged to meet Laura here? he wondered, then realised how foolish an idea that was in view of Laura's guest, although—when he looked—David could see no sign of the man.

He picked up his glass, wondering what had hap-

pened to him. Had the fellow left already or was he
joining Laura later? He was so caught up in trying to
work it out that he didn't realise Laura was speaking
to him until he heard her laugh.

'Penny for them? Although I'm sure that's not
enough. Thoughts *that* weighty must cost rather more!'

David summoned a smile, embarrassed to be caught
out that way. The last thing he wanted was for Laura
to suspect he was interested in her affairs. 'I was just
thinking about a patient I went to see on my way home.
It's one of those cases which you can't seem to get to
grips with.'

'Oh, why's that?' Laura sounded interested as she
picked up her glass of lemonade. David found himself
suddenly eager to tell her to see if she had any ideas
about Cyril's problems.

'The symptoms appear quite straightforward, but I
have this feeling that there's more to what's wrong
with him than meets the eye. He's suffering from a
general feeling of malaise and has lost considerable
weight, mainly because he vomits every time he eats.
I've also noticed that he seems to be cold all the time.'
David sighed as he reviewed Cyril's symptoms. 'I did
hope that it might be some sort of food poisoning but
it's been going on far too long for that.'

'How about his work? Could it be something he
comes into contact with on a daily basis, some sort of
chemical, perhaps?' Laura frowned. She seemed in-
trigued by the medical mystery. David found himself
thinking how good it was to have someone to talk to
about things like this. Oh, he could always consult one
of his partners about a case, and he did, but somehow
it was different to sit here with Laura and hear
her views.

'How about parathion poisoning?' she suggested, nibbling her lower lip with small white teeth as she mentally ran through all she knew about the condition. David looked away, staring down at the glass of shandy as he tried to control the sudden rush of emotions he felt. Did she have any idea how beautiful she was, how desirable? She must do, and yet she gave no indication of it as she continued in that same softly husky voice which had the power to turn his insides to water!

'Some of those organophosphate insecticides are very powerful. They can be absorbed through the skin as well as inhaled or swallowed. I imagine they use a lot of pesticides at the farms around here for all sorts of things.'

'Hmm, you're right, of course. And we do see cases of parathion poisoning from time to time, although, thankfully, people are far more aware of the dangers inherent in using the chemicals than they used to be.' David sighed. 'However, this patient isn't a farm worker. He works at the local pottery so he doesn't come into contact with insecticides, as so many people in Yewdale do. Also, the range of his symptoms isn't quite as far-reaching as parathion poisoning causes. There have been no headaches or blurred vision, no difficulty in breathing. It can't be that.'

'Then how about what he *does* come into contact with?' Laura leaned towards him and laid her hand on his arm. David knew she wasn't even aware of what she was doing but he still felt the jolt his body gave, the ripples of heat that ran through him in waves.

'You say he works at the pottery. Could it be lead poisoning? They use lead in the firing process, or so I believe. And with lead poisoning, it can build up over a period of time before it becomes a problem.'

David frowned, forcing himself to concentrate on what she'd said rather than on the host of emotions he felt. 'It's a good idea. We haven't had any incidences of lead poisoning in relation to the pottery but that doesn't mean it couldn't happen—' He broke off as Sam bent over to have a word.

'I hate to butt in, but Abbie and I are just off. We're going to a late-night show at the cinema over in Kendal.' Sam grimaced 'I rashly agreed to let her choose which film we saw so it's probably going to be some weepy!'

'Little do you know, sunshine!' Abbie retorted as she got up. 'You could be in for a big surprise. Don't blame me if you can't sleep tonight!' She turned and grinned at David and Laura. 'Have fun, you two.'

David shrugged, faintly uncomfortable with the way Abbie seemed determined to link him and Laura together. Obviously, Abbie had no idea that Laura had someone staying for the weekend, he thought, wondering why Laura hadn't mentioned her friend's visit. 'I'm on call, don't forget. In fact, I only came in for something to eat. Mike and Emily are staying with their grandmother and I couldn't be bothered to cook for myself.'

'Oh, what a shame!' Abbie exclaimed. 'There's no food on tonight. Rose has had to go somewhere so there was nobody to cook,' she explained, referring to Harry's wife, who did all the catering in the Fleece.

'Evidently there's been a problem with their son, Adrian, although Harry didn't seem inclined to go into any detail so I'm not sure what's happened. Adrian's been in a psychiatric unit and was due to come home shortly,' she added for Laura's benefit, before she grinned. 'Still, maybe someone will take pity on you, David, eh?'

Abbie shot a meaningful glance at Laura then followed Sam out of the pub. David picked up his glass, feeling the small silence which had fallen pressing in on him. It took him all his time to summon a smile when Frank and Jeannie announced that they were off as well. He could cheerfully have murdered Abbie for that last comment, well meant though it had been.

'I haven't eaten either, as it happens.' Laura drank the last drop of her lemonade and put the glass on the counter with a little click that made every nerve in David's body tauten. 'I've been sanding the sitting-room floor all day and came down to the Fleece to wash away the taste of sawdust, before making myself something. How about sharing a meal with me?'

David shook his head. 'No, it's fine, really...'

'Oh, come on! I'd love you to join me.' Laura laughed huskily. 'And it hasn't anything to do with the hints Abbie was throwing out either if that's what you're worried about!'

Once again he was disconcerted by her bluntness. Laura said all the things that other people simply skirted around. He gave a reluctant smile. 'It wasn't very subtle, was it? I'll have to have a word with Abbie when I see her next.'

'Don't! There's really no need, not when she meant well. I imagine she was only taking the view that most people around here have taken.' Laura got up and shrugged on her denim jacket. Once again it was overly large on her, the sleeves rolled up the requisite turns to free her hands. David found himself wondering whose jacket it was, then quickly clamped down on that thought, preferring not to know the answer.

He focused instead on that ambiguous comment she'd just made. 'What do you mean by that? What view have people taken?'

'Oh, only that you and I are an item, it seems!' She gave the softest chuckle as she saw his face. 'Oh, David, you must know what people are saying. It appears the whole town saw us driving over to Rowbottom Farm the other night!'

David put down his glass, aware that his hand wasn't quite steady. 'I'm sorry,' he began, only to break off as Laura laughed.

'Don't worry about it! I'm certainly not. Now, come along. I can't promise you anything more than a bowl of pasta but, although I say so myself, I *do* make the best pasta sauce you're likely to taste!'

She turned and headed for the door, leaving David little option but to follow her. His neck scorched as he felt people turning to watch them leave, and he realised that this was simply going to add fuel to the gossip. Laura was waiting for him outside, her collar turned up against the wind. She had her hands pushed into the pockets of her jacket and her shoulders hunched. Her blonde hair was escaping from the knot into which she'd fastened it, and silky wisps blew across her cheeks. She brushed them back with an impatient hand, frowning as David hesitated.

'Nothing wrong, is there? Don't tell me you don't like pasta?' There was a teasing lightness to the words and yet it couldn't quite disguise the undercurrent in her voice. David's heart skipped one beat, then a second and started to race to make up for lost time. He turned to look along the road as he tried to get a grip on himself, but it seemed that his mind was buzzing with far too many thoughts and ideas to make that possible.

What harm would it do to accept the invitation? the voice of temptation whispered silkily. It was just an invitation to a meal, nothing more—no strings attached to it, surely? Yet he still held back.

'David?'

There was now uncertainty in Laura's voice, a suggestion of hurt which stung him into action far quicker than anything else could have done. 'Look, I don't think it's a good idea to let people start thinking that you and I—that we—' He broke off, unable to make himself utter the words out loud. He took a deep breath and tried again. 'Anyway, I thought you had somebody staying with you?' he said flatly.

'Good heavens, I didn't realise the grapevine was that good!' Laura laughed in amazement. She brushed back a long strand of hair which had caught across her mouth and smiled at him. 'Anyhow, Adam's gone now. He left this afternoon once he'd made sure I wouldn't kill myself using the floor-sanding machine. It took me all my time to persuade him that I was perfectly capable of using it without my big brother's supervision!'

'Brother… You mean he was—is—your brother?' David heard the relief in his voice and knew that Laura had heard it too when her smile abruptly faded.

'Yes. Adam is my brother—well, one of them. He's a year older than I am, which makes him thirty-six.' Laura took a deep breath, her pretty face unusually sober in the light spilling through the pub's windows. 'Why? Who did you think he was, David?'

CHAPTER SIX

DAVID took a small breath simply because he couldn't manage a larger one. Laura was looking at him with those clear blue eyes as she waited for an answer…

'Friend, colleague, lover.' He shrugged, striving for a nonchalance he didn't feel. Why did he suddenly want to start turning cartwheels in the middle of the street because Adam had turned out to be Laura's brother?

'I see.' Laura stood up straighter, not that she was anywhere near approaching his eye level, David realised. Yet she still managed to command his attention, the light in her blue eyes making it impossible for him to look away.

'And how do you feel now that you know that Adam isn't a friend or a colleague…or my lover?' She laid the tiniest emphasis on the last word but it was enough to send a wash of heat through his veins. David would have given anything he owned to be able to avoid the question, but it was impossible when Laura stood there, so small and straight as she stared him in the eye and demanded that he tell her the truth.

'Relieved.'

His tone was curt almost to the point of rudeness, but Laura didn't blink. She simply nodded her silky blonde head, abruptly turned on her heel and started walking along the street.

David stood where he was for a moment before he suddenly came to his senses and hurried after her. His long legs covered the distance in a few strides, but Laura didn't glance at him as he walked along beside her. They carried on like that for several minutes until the silence began to grate on his nerves. It was too unsettling, too dangerous, too…too full of all sorts of things!

'Laura?' There was a question in his voice but she didn't look round. He could hear the rapid sound of her breathing as she strode briskly on. They turned down the lane towards their houses and still she didn't say anything or even look at him. He caught hold of her arm, bringing her to an abrupt halt as he swung her round to face him. 'What is it? Tell me.'

Her eyes were cloudy blue, the shadows stealing all the brightness from them as they searched his face. 'You won't like it if I tell you, David.'

He felt every muscle in his body react to the words so that a spasm ran through him, and he knew she'd felt it because her small body stiffened. His voice sounded hoarse because it was so difficult to push any words past the lump in his throat. 'Why do you say that?'

Unwittingly his hands slid up her arms under the loose sleeves of her jacket, his fingers caressing the smooth, warm flesh he found underneath. Satiny, silky, soft, warm… His mind ran riot with a host of adjectives which didn't come anywhere near to describing how Laura's skin felt to him. His fingers loosely circled her wrists while he marvelled at their fragility.

'Tell me, Laura…please.'

Her eyes closed for a moment, before opening to look straight into his. 'I was pleased that you felt re-lieved about who Adam is. It means that you feel something for me, David, although…although I know that you don't want to.'

His hands tightened, his fingers biting into her for a moment before he realised what he was doing and let her go. He felt so mixed up that it was little wonder he had difficulty putting his feelings into words. 'I don't know how to explain… It isn't easy, Laura. There's Kate, and I feel so…'

'Guilty?' She laughed gently as she lifted her hand and touched his cheek. 'Do you think I don't know that, David? Do you imagine that I don't understand what you're going through? That's why it scares me so much.'

'Scares you?' he said blankly, feeling the gentle pressure of her fingers against his cheek.

'To know that I could so easily fall in love with you if I let myself.'

'I…' He didn't know what to say once again because there simply weren't any words for this sort of situation. He looked into Laura's beautiful face and felt the ache start deep inside him. It was a mixture of longing and pain, joy and fear, and it almost brought him to his knees.

Laura reached up on tiptoe and pressed her mouth to his in the briefest of kisses imaginable before she stepped back. 'Maybe we should take a rain check on that dinner, David. I don't think either of us could handle it right now, and I'd hate for us to do anything which we might come to regret.'

David felt his blood race as he understood her meaning only too well. If he went back to Laura's house, it wouldn't be only dinner they'd share! God, he could imagine it now, having her in his arms and making love to her until both of them were dizzy…

And he could imagine how he'd feel later when it hit him what he'd done.

Laura gave him a sad, knowing smile then hurried away. David watched her turn into her gate and heard Peebody bark a joyful greeting as she opened the door. His hands clenched as he fought against the urge to follow her and knock on her door.

He tipped his head back and stared up at the sky, seeing the stars through a haze of despair. Nothing seemed harder than going back inside his own house to be greeted by the emptiness and silence, but he had to do it. He couldn't take what Laura would give so willingly, knowing that he'd only end up by hurting her.

Laura deserved more than that. She deserved a man who could love her with the whole of his heart—without reservations, without regrets, without guilt. He wasn't that man, although by heaven he wished he was!

The evening dragged past. David made himself a sandwich then left it untouched. He couldn't face food. He switched on the television but after a few minutes turned it off. He didn't want to watch television. He turned on the stereo and even tried listening to one of Mike's CDs. It was loud and filled the silence, which was the best he could say for it.

He switched it off, letting the silence fall back into place as he roamed from room to room. His mind was in turmoil, his body not much better. He ached in ways he hadn't ached in years.

He strode to the window, but all it took was a glimpse of the light shining in the bedroom of the house next door to make him realise that it wasn't a good idea. He didn't need to torment himself with images of Laura in her lonely bed, for heaven's sake!

In a final fit of impatience he went upstairs to bed himself, although it was barely ten o'clock. He took a shower then slid into pyjama pants and glanced at the telephone on the bedside table, willing it to ring. What he needed was a call to take his mind off all these thoughts that plagued him.

His gaze moved to the photo beside the telephone, and his heart ached as he picked it up. Kate's face stared back at him but suddenly he could hardly bear to look at the lifeless image. In the first few months after her death he'd simply closed his eyes and Kate had flowed into his mind—her scent, her laughter, the way she'd had of tilting her head when she'd looked at him, all the hundred and one little things that had made her who she was.

Now it was an effort to recall the details that once had been so familiar, and it hurt to know that she was fading away from him. It was the healing process, his mind coming to terms with the loss because nobody could endure such constant pain, but it all served to increase his sense of guilt. He *should* be able to remember everything about her so much better!

David put the picture down and switched off the lamp. Punching the pillow into shape, he closed his eyes then found them flying open again as he heard a noise outside. He stared into the darkness, listening so hard that he could hear his own heart thumping against the mattress.

There it was again—the soft but unmistakable sound of footsteps.

He got out of bed and went to the window, but it was too dark to see anything in the garden. There was no light on in the house next door now either, and the tiny sliver of moon was too weak to make much impression. The footsteps were suddenly louder, crunching on the gravel as someone came up the path to his door. David found himself holding his breath, but the bell didn't ring...

He was out of the room and down the stairs at a run, flicking on the landing light as he went. There had been a couple of break-ins in the area recently and his house was quite isolated. He hauled open the front door then gasped as a huge, dark shape launched itself at him. Before he knew what was happening he found himself in a heap on the floor, trying to evade what felt very much like a dog's tongue lavishing attention on him he could have done without!

'What the devil...?' he spluttered.

'Peebody! Oh, you bad dog! Look what you've done!'

Laura sounded truly concerned as she hauled the excited dog off him. David struggled to his feet and ran a hand over his face, grimacing as he felt the wetness on his jaw. The damned dog had very nearly licked him to death, he thought. Then his attention was diverted to the dog's owner...

'What's going on?' he demanded with as much authority as he could muster, which was pitifully little. He fixed his gaze on Laura's face, trying to ignore the sound of hollow laughter inside his head. Did he *honestly* believe that if he kept his eyes focused above her shoulder level then it wouldn't cause him the least problem that Laura was standing on his step dressed only in a thigh-length nightshirt and equally short towelling robe?

His body gave its own verdict on that idea, summing

it up along the lines of a nice try but not very effective. David kept his gaze firmly fixed on her face, praying that his loose pyjama bottoms wouldn't reveal too many secrets!

'I'm sorry, David. I wasn't sure whether to knock or not, but Peebody took the decision out of my hands.' Laura bent and shook an admonishing finger at the dog. 'Bad boy! Fancy knocking David over like that, you great goon.

'I hope he didn't hurt you, David,' she continued in concern, her eyes drifting upwards as she checked him over for any obvious signs of injury. Her gaze lingered just for a second more than it should have around the level of his hips, before winging to his face as faint colour tinted her cheeks.

'No, just gave me a shock, that's all.' His voice sounded faintly strangled and he cleared his throat, but it didn't ease the discomfort he felt, either physical or mental. His mind and body were in cahoots—one conjuring up delectable images, the other reacting to them!

'What were you doing, anyway?' he asked, to cover another wave of confusion and good old-fashioned lust.

'My lights have fused. I was checking to see if I had a torch in the car when Peebody made a dash for safety.' She gave a strained laugh, obviously determined to handle the situation with aplomb. 'This cowardly animal is terrified of the dark. I have to leave a night-light on for him, would you believe?'

David laughed at the idea and the moment of tension passed. 'Worse than a baby, isn't he? Anyway, did you manage to sort out what the trouble was?'

'No. I didn't get a chance. Mind you, it looks as though all the fuses have blown so it must be something major. I think I'd be better off getting an electri-

cian in tomorrow rather than go poking around myself
when I know zilch about electrical circuits. I expect the
wiring needs renewing. It's certainly old enough,'
Laura sighed. 'Anyway, it does leave me with a bit of
a problem. I hate to ask, but is there any chance that
Peebody could stay here with you tonight? He'll never
settle if the house is in darkness, but he'll be fine in
the kitchen here so long as you leave a light on for
him.'

'Of course. Bring him in—' David broke off with a
grin as the dog dashed past him. 'I think he understood
what you said.'

Laura laughed throatily. 'Probably! Anyhow, I really
am sorry to have disturbed you like this. I'll pick
Peebody up in the morning, if that's OK with you.
Goodnight.'

She turned to go but David stopped her. 'Wait! You
can't stay by yourself in the dark. You could trip over
something and hurt yourself.'

She shrugged as she glanced back. 'It's a bit late to
start looking for somewhere tonight. I'll be fine, honestly. I've got the torch and that's all I need.'

Once again she started to leave but David knew he
wouldn't have a minute's peace, thinking about her all
alone in the house without any lights. 'Look, you can
stay here for the night. You can have Emily's room.'

'Well, I don't know…' Her uncertainty was obvious,
as was the reason for it. David knew it was down to
him to convince her.

'Please, stay here tonight, Laura.' He took a deep
breath. 'After all, what are friends for if not to help
each other out in situations like this?'

She gave him a slow smile but the expression in her
eyes told him that she understood what he was saying,

that he was laying down boundaries to their relationship. David found himself holding his breath as he waited to hear what she'd say. Suddenly it seemed vitally important that she accept what he was offering her, no matter that it was so little and probably not what either of them really wanted. To have Laura as a friend was better than nothing, though.

'Thank you. I…I'm grateful for the offer.' She gave a soft laugh, obviously trying to inject a touch of lightness into the sombre mood. 'I have to confess that I didn't relish the thought of staying on my own in the pitch dark. I'm almost as much of a coward as Peebody is when it comes to the thought of mice scuttling about!'

'I'm sure they'd be far more scared of you, but I know what you mean.' David was pleased with the level tone of his voice as she stepped inside the hall. He closed the door then felt his heart start to pound as he turned round. Laura was standing in the middle of the hall, looking so small and defenceless in her nightclothes, with her soft blonde curls tumbling around her face.

His hands clenched because the urge to reach out and touch her was almost irresistible—only that wasn't what friends did, was it? Friends offered tea and sympathy and warm beds for the night. They provided shoulders to cry on and words of encouragement. Those were the guidelines but could he stick to them? Could he manage to keep this beautiful, warm, *sexy* woman as a friend? Or would the temptation to take their relationship one step further prove too great to resist…?

'It's a good job Emily isn't here or she might start

thinking all the hints she's been dropping have had the desired effect.'

David blinked as he realised what Laura had said. 'What do you mean?' He suddenly remembered what had been plaguing him all week. 'What has Emily been up to? You mentioned something along those lines the other day on the phone.'

'Oh, not a lot.' Laura laughed as she ran her hand over her soft halo of curls, ruffling them even more. 'Just dropping the odd remark into the conversation about how nice her daddy is and how she wishes he'd get married again. Oh, and there was the bit about how *much* he loves dogs, of course. Although maybe that needs reviewing in the light of Peebody's performance tonight.'

'I don't know what to say...' David felt so embarrassed that he wished the ground would open up beneath him. It was just as he'd feared—and worse!

'Don't worry about it!' Laura laughed at his stricken expression. 'I think it's wonderful that Emily loves you so much that she cares like that. You're a very lucky man to have a daughter like Emily, David Ross, so count your blessings. And all we need to do is make sure that she understands the situation.'

'About us just being friends, you mean?'

'Of course. There's no point in raising Emily's hopes, only to have her disappointed, is there?' Laura gave him one last smile then made her way along the hall. David could hear her talking to the dog, although he couldn't make out what she was actually saying.

He took a deep breath like a swimmer coming up for air. Just friends. It would *have* to be enough—for all of them!

*   *   *

'David? David…wake up.'

The sweet voice filtered into his dream and David smiled. In his mind's eye he could see the sun coming up over the horizon, a hazy wash of gold that turned the lush countryside to a place of unbelievable beauty. He could hardly believe the colours of the flowers or the scent of their perfume—

'David?'

That voice again, as low and sweet as a musical interlude. David turned his head towards it, his smile widening as a woman's face came into view—blue eyes, tumbling blonde curls. She bent towards him, her lips parting on a soft sigh as they hovered above his—

'David!'

He came awake with a rush, his heart pounding as he sat up and cannoned into the small figure bending over him. Laura tried to avoid the contact but ended up overbalancing instead. Instinctively his hands shot out to steady her, but he was a shade too late as she landed on the bed beside him in a flurry of bare legs and cotton nightshirt.

'Are you OK?' His voice grated with concern and sleep and a lot of other things he preferred not to put a name to.

'Yes, fine. My foot sort of slipped.' Laura rolled onto her side with a laugh. 'I hope I didn't squash you.'

David shook his head, trying to ignore the way it felt to have her small body pressed all down the length of his. The intimacy of their position made his head reel with ideas he knew he shouldn't be having in view of their previous pact.

A *real* friend shouldn't feel this desire to draw Laura into his arms and hold her close, shouldn't long to bury his face in the sweetly scented hollow of her neck, shouldn't ache to feel her warmth stealing into all the cold, lonely corners of his heart...

'I'm fine,' he managed to say through gritted teeth, but he realised that Laura had sensed how far from 'fine' he really was because she quickly rolled to her feet and smoothed her nightshirt over her bare thighs.

'You must have been fast asleep,' she said huskily, in a voice that told him she wasn't immune to the situation either. 'I called you at least a dozen times but you didn't hear me.'

'I didn't.' David ran his hand over his face and tried taking a few deep breaths, but they weren't overly successful in calming his jumping nerves. He glanced at the clock—anything to avoid looking at Laura—and blinked as he saw the time. Four o'clock? In the morning?

'You obviously didn't hear the phone ringing either. Here you are.' Laura handed him a neatly written message slip, cutting short any notions he had about why she'd seen fit to wake him at this hour. David sighed as he glanced at the paper, knowing he should be glad, not disappointed, that Laura was acting strictly within the guidelines he'd laid down. Just friends...nothing more.

'Can you read my writing all right?' Laura bent to read the message over his shoulder and David felt his pulse leap as he caught the warm scent of her skin. He stared at the slip of paper until the words blurred, jolting back to the present only when Laura began reading them out to him.

'It was a Mrs Rimmer who called. She said that she lives in the high street. Evidently one of her guests has been taken ill, and can you come straight away?'

'Did she give you any details?' David queried, tossing back the bedclothes.

'Not really, just that the lady had been taken poorly and needed to see a doctor. I think she was worried in case I didn't pass the message on to you because she asked me several times who I was,' Laura explained, before she turned to leave the room.

'I see.' David dragged a sweater over his head then ran his hand over his hair to smooth it down. 'Thanks, Laura. I'm sorry you were woken up. I never heard the phone at all.'

'Don't worry about it.' Laura stopped to glance back. David felt his mouth go dry as he saw how the light from the landing had turned her nightshirt semi-transparent. Through it he could just make out the soft, lush curves of her body...

He turned away to pick up the trousers he'd left over the back of a chair and his tone was slightly gruff. 'Well, thanks anyway. I do appreciate it.'

'As you said yourself, David, what are friends for?'

She was gone in a trice, closing the door quietly behind her. David stepped into his trousers, wondering if there had been the faintest hint of challenge in that final statement.

He sighed as he slid his feet into his shoes. Probably! It didn't take a genius to work out that whatever he felt for Laura went beyond the boundaries of friendship.

Peebody thumped his tail on the floor to let David know that he'd seen him when he went into the kitchen to collect his keys. His duty done, the dog closed his eyes again with a contented sigh, leaving the humans to go racing about in the middle of the night.

David laughed to himself as he quietly shut the

kitchen door, leaving the light over the counter switched on. No point in spoiling Peebody's sleep! he thought wryly. Although he could hardly believe that he'd slept through the sound of the phone ringing so that Laura had had to answer it...

He groaned as it suddenly hit him that now the whole town would know she'd spent the night at his house. Marion Rimmer was the local busybody so any hope they'd had of keeping it quiet was out of the question. Maybe he and Laura knew that nothing had gone on but would anyone believe that? Oh, hell!

'Sounds real funny, she does, Dr Ross, all slurred and strange-like. I asked her if she wanted a drink of tea but I couldn't make head nor tail of what she was trying to tell me. It was just lucky that I heard her moaning, otherwise she could have been like that all night long.'

Marion Rimmer spoke in a hushed tone as she led the way up the narrow staircase. She ran one of the small bed and breakfast establishments on the high street and had warned David when she opened the door that she didn't want her other guests disturbed.

He followed her into the dimly lit room and went straight to the old-fashioned bed, bending to speak to the elderly lady who was lying in it. 'Hello, Mrs Chadwick, I'm Dr Ross. Mrs Rimmer tells me that you aren't feeling very well so I'd just like to examine you, if that's all right.'

The woman tried to say something but it was impossible to make out what it was. David noticed that one corner of her mouth was drooping slightly and that her face was very flushed. He set his case down then took her pulse and found it very heavy and rapid.

'What is it, Dr Ross? Do you know?' Marion
Rimmer demanded from her position by the door. A
widow in her early sixties, Marion thrived on gossip.
David knew that a lot of the rumours that surfaced in
the town came from her lips so he preferred not to
discuss the patient's illness with her if he could avoid
it.

'I'll know better once I've finished examining Mrs
Chadwick. Is she staying here on her own?' he asked
instead.

'Oh, no. She has a friend with her, another lady.
She's in the front bedroom, paid extra for the *en suite*
facilities, you see.'

'Then I wonder if you could go and knock on her
door, Mrs Rimmer? It would be a help if I could speak
to her, and she's bound to want to know that her friend
isn't well.'

'I didn't think it necessary to bother her, but if you
think I should...' Marion reluctantly went away to
wake Mrs Chadwick's friend when David nodded. He
returned to the task of examining his patient, although
he was already ninety per cent certain what was wrong
with her.

'I'm just going to take a look in your eyes, Mrs
Chadwick. It's nothing to be alarmed about so just lie
still.'

Gently lifting the old lady's eyelids, he could see
immediately that her pupils were unevenly dilated. He
sighed as he realised that his suspicions were correct.
He was certain now that Mrs Chadwick had suffered a
stroke as she was exhibiting all the symptoms.

'Elsie!' Another elderly woman suddenly appeared,
her face crumpling as she saw her friend lying on the
bed. 'Oh!'

David went over and gently drew her out onto the landing. 'I take it that you're Mrs Chadwick's friend?'

'Yes. Hilda Dale. What's wrong with her, Doctor? She looks so ill!' A sob caught in her throat and David patted her arm, wishing there was an easy way to break the bad news to her.

'I'm very sorry, Mrs Dale, but it seems that Mrs Chadwick has had a stroke from the look of her.'

'A stroke? Oh, no!' Tears welled from the elderly lady's eyes. She found a tissue in the pocket of her dressing-gown and dabbed at them. 'But she's always been so fit, so…so well!'

'I'm sure she has.' David sighed. 'Sometimes there are warning signs and sometimes it can happen seemingly out of the blue, as in this case. However, what we need to do now is to get Mrs Chadwick to the hospital straight away. They will be able to determine the best course of treatment for your friend.'

'But will she be all right? Elsie has always been such a strong woman. I've seen people who've had strokes and they're never the same afterwards, are they?'

'I'm afraid it's impossible to tell how much damage has been done at the moment. It will take a while to see how much of the brain has been affected,' David explained quietly. 'All I can say is that a lot of patients make excellent recoveries. Let's just hope that Mrs Chadwick falls into that category.'

Leaving Mrs Dale to sit with her friend, David went downstairs and rang for an ambulance. Marion Rimmer came along the hall with a cup of tea on a tray just as he'd finished, and he realised he had no choice but to explain the situation to her.

'Well, I never did! Fit as a fiddle she seemed, too. A stroke, you say, Dr Ross? And how bad is it?'

Marion Rimmer's eyes gleamed with interest and David bit back a few sharp words as he imagined her regaling everyone in the town with what had gone on that night. It wasn't that she was really unkind, simply insensitive.

'We won't know until she's seen by a consultant. He'll arrange for Mrs Chadwick to have a brain scan to assess the damage.' He looked pointedly at the cooling cup of tea. 'I'm sure Mrs Dale will be glad of that. She seems very upset.'

'I'll take it up to her now.' Marion started towards the stairs then paused. 'I hope I didn't wake everyone up when I rang your house tonight, Dr Ross. And you with guests staying over, too. Sounded very efficient, the young lady who answered, but she said she was a doctor so I expect she's used to being woken up through the night.'

'I'm sure Dr Mackenzie has done her share of night calls, Mrs Rimmer,' David replied dryly, realising that there was no point in pretending that Laura hadn't been there. It would have to be a damage limitation exercise from here on in, although whether the story would gain its own momentum as it circulated was something he could do little about.

'Dr Mackenzie had a bit of trouble with the electricity in her house tonight. All the lights fused so I offered her somewhere to stay for the night,' he explained blandly. 'It seemed the neighbourly thing to do.'

'Oh, of course! It was a good job you were able to help her out, Dr Ross.' Marion smiled smugly. 'And, of course, there was no need for me to go worrying about waking the children up, was there? I saw them going off with their grandma just before tea tonight. Young Emily told me that they were staying the weekend with her now that I think on. There was only you and Dr Mackenzie in the house tonight so I don't feel half so bad about ringing now.'

Marion sedately carried on up the stairs. David raised his eyes to the heavens. What was that bit in the Hippocratic oath about causing no harm by deliberate intent? He'd never felt more sorely tempted to break it. Give it two days maximum and the news that Laura Mackenzie had spent the night with him would be all round Cumbria never mind Yewdale!

CHAPTER SEVEN

THE tantalising aroma of bacon frying greeted David as he opened the front door. He'd waited for the ambulance to arrive to take Elsie Chadwick to hospital but it was still barely six a.m. He frowned as he put his case down on the hall table. What was Laura doing up at this time of the morning?

He made his way to the kitchen and stood in the doorway, simply enjoying the scene. Laura was standing by the stove, expertly turning an egg in the hot fat. She had her hair tucked behind her ears and her face was sightly flushed from the heat of the stove. The short towelling robe was firmly wrapped around her small body, the belt tied in a workmanlike knot which made David's breath catch as he imagined how it would be to untie it...

She must have realised she was being watched because she suddenly glanced round. Her lips parted in a little moue of surprise as she saw him, then she grinned. 'Caught me!'

His brows rose as he leaned against the doorframe. It had been so long since a woman had made breakfast in this kitchen that he didn't want to miss a moment of the experience. Kate's illness had meant that she'd been unable to do much around the house in the months leading up to her death so David had taken over the cooking himself and had hired someone to do the cleaning.

As he watched Laura working away, it filled him

with a mix of emotions and yet the strongest of them all was simple pleasure at seeing her there. She looked so *right*, standing before the stove in his house—although that was hardly the most politically correct thought he'd ever come up with!

'You don't mind, do you?' There was sudden uncertainty on Laura's face as he continued to stand there without uttering a word. David put his mind back into gear, trying to make it go forward this time not back to such purely male and utterly neolithic thoughts!

'Of course I don't mind. You must know that you're free to help yourself to anything you want,' he said with a coolness he dearly wished he felt.

'Thanks. I was absolutely starving, to tell the truth, which was why I couldn't sleep.' Her eyes, as blue and deep as the ocean, swung round to his. 'I made myself a sandwich last night when I got in, but I never ate it.'

Those blue eyes moved deliberately to the counter where David had left his own uneaten sandwich and she gave a little laugh. 'Seems like neither of us had much of an appetite last night after all so how about sharing this with me instead?'

David shrugged, not sure how it made him feel to hear her admit that she'd been as mixed up as he'd been last night. 'Sure. If there's enough.'

'Loads! My cooking tends to be on the generous side. Comes from being one of a large family.' Laura laughed as she divided the mound of crisp bacon between two plates then added heaped spoonfuls of tomatoes and an egg each. She set both plates on the table then went to get the cutlery out of the drawer, seemingly having no difficulty finding her way around the strange kitchen.

She sat down and took her first bite of bacon, rolling

Get up to two **FREE** books, plus TWO bonus gifts! When you play...

The LUCKY STARS GAME

HOW TO PLAY:

★ Carefully scratch away the silver circle. Then match the star sign revealed to those opposite to find out how many gifts we have for you!

★ When you send back the card you will receive specially selected Mills & Boon® Medical Romance™ novels. These books have a cover price of at least £2.40 each, but they are yours to keep absolutely free.

★ There's no catch. You're under no obligation to buy anything. We charge you nothing for you're first shipment. And you don't have to make any minimum number of purchases.

★ The fact is thousands of readers enjoy receiving books through the post from the Reader Service™. They like the convenience of home delivery… they like gettin the best new novels befor they're available in the shops… and they love their subscriber Newsletter, featuring author news, horoscopes, competitions and much more!

★ We hope that you'll want to remain a subscriber. But the choice yours – to continue or cancel, anytin at all. So why not take up our invitation, with no risk of any kind. You'll be glad you did!

NO COST! NO RISK! NO OBLIGATION TO BUY!

--------- ◆ DETACH AND POST CARD TODAY. NO STAMP NEEDED! ◆ ---------

The Reader Service ™
FREEPOST CN81
Croydon
Surrey
CR9 3WZ

NO
STAMP
NEEDED

her eyes with pleasure. 'Mmm, at least a month's worth
of cholesterol, but what the heck? This is *really* good,
though I say so myself!'

David laughed as he tucked in. 'It is. But what was
that about a large family—do you have many brothers
and sisters, then?'

'Uh-huh,' Laura muttered, her mouth full of tomatoes. She delicately wiped a smear of tomato off her
upper lip with a piece of kitchen roll, which was all
she'd been able to find to serve as napkins.

David quickly looked away as he struggled to control the rush of desire he felt. What wouldn't he give
to have done that for her, to have removed that tiny
smudge from her lip with his tongue before letting it
trace that perfect Cupid's bow?

His hands clenched as a wave of amazement rocked
him. When had he *ever* imagined doing such a thing
before? he wondered dazedly. When had something
so...so insignificant as a woman wiping her mouth put
such *lustful* ideas into his head?

Never. The answer came back loud and clear. Not
once in the whole of his adult life had it happened. It
stunned him to admit it, made him instantly feel guilty
and afraid. What was happening to him? Why was he
acting like this? Why did he feel things for Laura he
hadn't even felt for Kate?

'There were five of us—four boys and me—so, as
you can imagine, my mother spent a great deal of her
time in the kitchen. And because she was there we all
seemed to gravitate towards that room. I think it was
a process of osmosis—we simply absorbed how to
cook without being aware of it!' Laura laughed remi-
niscently as she picked up a strip of crispy bacon.
Snapping it in two, she tossed a piece to Peebody, who

was waiting politely by her chair. He swallowed it in a single gulp then turned hopeful eyes in David's direction.

It was an effort to concentrate on what Laura was saying but David tried his best—anything that would stop his mind wandering along paths it had never trodden before. He cut a strip of bacon into two and gave half to the dog, who rewarded him with a thump of his tail.

'Sounds as though you were very close,' he said quietly, watching Laura's face so that he saw the fleeting expression of sadness that crossed it.

'We were. My father died when I was quite small so I don't remember him at all. Mum brought us up by herself. It must have been a struggle because there were so many of us and she did a part-time job as well, cleaning at a local cinema each morning.

'I don't suppose there was much money either, but none of us were aware of that. She was always there when we needed her, ready to listen and give advice or simply let us work out what to do. She died not long after I qualified. She was so proud of all of us and I was very glad that she knew I had kept up the tradition.'

'Tradition?'

'Of going into medicine.' Laura laughed when she saw that he didn't understand. 'All five of us studied medicine. Oh, we went to different universities but I imagine it's still a record to have so many members of one family go into the same profession.'

'It must be,' David shook his head in bemusement. 'So where do your brothers practice?'

'The twins, Michael and Philip, are GPs with their own practice in Derbyshire. Stephen's a professor now, much in demand lecturing in his field, which is lung cancer. And Adam has just come back from working in the States. He was on an exchange visit to Boston. His speciality is trauma care. He trains other doctors working in emergency units in advanced trauma life support.

'His aim is to make sure that every doctor in that field has an ATLS certificate, but it isn't easy getting it across to health authorities how vital such training is.'

'It's amazing, all five of you...!' David shook his head. 'Your mother must have been very proud of you all.'

'She was, although she would have been equally as proud if we'd worked in an office or a bank or whatever.' Laura got up to pour them both coffee, automatically sidestepping Peebody. 'She was a wonderful mother and we were very lucky to have her.'

'I always think that about my kids, how lucky they were to have had Kate—' David broke off. He felt suddenly uncomfortable about saying that to Laura and uneasy about why he should feel that way.

'They were.' Laura brought the coffee back and sat down again. 'I can tell that from what Emily says. Kate must have been a wonderful mother and a lovely person, too. I get this warm feeling whenever Emily or Mike mention her name.'

Tears stung David's eyes and he stared down at his coffee. 'She was. It was so unfair, her dying like that...' He couldn't continue as the tears clogged his throat. He wasn't aware of Laura getting up until he felt her arms go around him as she drew his head to her breast and held him.

'You shouldn't keep it bottled up like that, David. I

know how it's been—you wanted to be strong for the sake of the children—but it's all right to feel angry and sad. Kate was taken from you and it *was* unfair!'

Her hand smoothed his hair, her touch as light as a breeze. David could feel the full force of the emotions he'd kept pent up inside him all these months suddenly exploding. He pressed his face into Laura's softness, unashamed of his grief or that she should witness it. If it had to be anyone he broke down in front of then it was right it should be her.

It took some time for the storm to abate. Laura held him the whole time, her hand stroking his hair and his face, her soft voice murmuring words he couldn't hear yet which soothed him. He drew back at last, seeing the compassion in her eyes, the tenderness in the smile she gave him. She was so beautiful and caring, so much of a woman, that he'd have been less of a man himself if he hadn't been aware of that.

His hands slid behind her back as he drew her to him, feeling the warmth that flowed through his body as he felt her softness come to rest against him once more. She was so tiny that even sitting down his mouth was on a level with her neck, and it was simply irresistible to feel the smoothness of her skin against his lips and not do anything about it...

His lips skimmed the delicate column, tasting, testing. He felt her shiver yet he knew that she wasn't cold. His heart began to pound so hard that he could feel it shaking his body and knew that Laura could feel it to.

'David.' She took his face between her hands, her eyes luminous as they held his, and he felt every muscle in his body tauten as he saw what they held—the invitation, the giving, the need.

He wasn't even aware of standing up but suddenly

he was on his feet and his arms were around her once more. This time he had to bend to find her mouth but she met him halfway, going up on tiptoe so that their lips met with a small jolt.

There was nothing smooth and polished about the contact but, then, this was real life not a fairy story. In stories the hero swept the beautiful heroine into his arms and their first kiss was a masterpiece of seduction, not this explosive contact that generated a blazing urgency and made both of them clumsy with need. Their lips fumbled for a moment before suddenly they found just the right way to blend...

David's head swam. He could see stars dancing before his eyes and let his lids close, but he could still see their brilliance. Every single cliché shot into his head at that moment—from surf pounding to rockets going off—and not one of them summed up the rush of emotions he felt.

Laura's lips were warm and soft and so utterly desirable that he could have stood there until he died, just letting himself enjoy their taste and feel. It was only when she gave the softest murmur and moved against him that shocked delight gave way to a hungry desire that gnawed at his insides. Suddenly, to hold Laura in his arms and kiss her wasn't enough.

His hands gripped her upper arms, although whether to draw her closer or push her away David wasn't sure. His blood was racing and his brain too, the signals it was giving out all mixed up. It was only when Laura gave a strained laugh that he was suddenly able to breathe again.

'This can go one of two ways,' she murmured, her eyes holding his. 'And it can be whatever you want it to be, David, because there won't be any strings.'

Could he do it? Could he accept this gift she was offering him, the comfort—hell, that wasn't the word— of her body, without it tearing him in two afterwards? Could he refuse when he was aching for her in places he hadn't known he possessed until now? The decision was the hardest one he'd ever had to make.

Laura drew back abruptly, obviously taking his silence for her answer. There was a rigidity to the set of her narrow shoulders as she drew herself up, a twist to her soft mouth that spoke of pain even though she refused to show it. 'I'd better get back home. Thanks for putting me up for the night, David. I appreciate it.'

She held out her hand, obviously wanting him to know that she understood that their relationship was back on the old footing. How he wished *he* did, though!

As his fingers closed around her slender ones, David felt the surge of raw desire once more. He drew her to him with a speed that brought a gasp from her lips, but there was no more protest as he bent and covered her mouth with his in a kiss that said everything he couldn't. When he swept her up into his arms her arm looped around his neck as though it had done it a thousand times before, and desire was suddenly tempered by tenderness as he carried her towards the stairs.

Whatever he felt for Laura Mackenzie it wasn't just lust. It was a lot more than that, although he wasn't ready to admit what it was just yet... He felt a sharp stab of pain. Maybe he never would be ready but he couldn't deal with that thought now.

It was like his dream, only better. Morning sunlight filtered into the room, gilding the bed with soft light as he laid Laura down on it. She gave him a small, almost tentative smile but there was no hesitation about the way she held her arms out to him.

David sat on the edge of the mattress and bent to rain a shower of kisses over her delicate face. She gave a small murmur of pleasure, her body arching so that it brushed against his. Lifting her hands, she brought them around his neck and held him while she scattered kisses over his face, and David felt the heavy beat of his heart grow heavier still. His chest felt as though it would burst from the pressure as he drew back and their eyes met...

Laura's hands went to the belt of her robe but David gently pushed them away. 'No, let me do that.'

His voice sounded raw, resonating with the welter of emotions he felt, but, then, the very air around them seemed charged with emotion at that moment. It was such a small action yet such a huge step so that his hands shook as he untied the belt and parted her robe...

He felt as though he'd been poleaxed as he discovered that she wasn't wearing anything under it. His eyes flew to hers and he saw the blush that tinted her creamy skin with rosy colour.

'I had a shower and it didn't seem worth putting my nightshirt back on...' Her voice trailed away, her eyes watching his face as though she were afraid he might not like what he saw. David almost laughed out loud at that idea, but he didn't have enough energy to spare for anything more than simply enjoying the perfection of her small body as she lay there bathed in the golden light.

She was exquisite, he thought giddily, each soft curve, each hollow. His eyes skimmed from her collarbone to the surprisingly lush fullness of her breasts and almost stopped there, before reluctantly moving on to drink in the rest of her. Her waist was tiny, her hips trim, and her slender legs ended in the daintiest pair of feet he'd ever seen, her toenails polished with a pale rose pink. Laura was everything a man could have hoped for and David felt his body respond with blatant appreciation.

He kissed her again with hungry urgency this time, and felt her unstinting response. That seemed to set loose the very last reservation he had. It took only seconds to drag his sweater over his head, shed his trousers and the rest of his clothes. Laura's eyes were intent as they ran over his body so that David felt a momentary qualm. What if she were disappointed by what she saw? What if…?

Her hand rose to his chest, her fingers twining in the crisp dark hair that covered it. 'Make love to me, David…please.'

There was no disappointment in her voice and none in her brilliant blue eyes as they rose to his. David felt ten feet tall as he saw the desire in them and knew that it was solely for him. Suddenly, where once he had fumbled and been unsure, his every move became masterful and adept so that he smiled as he heard the gasp that left her lips as his hand swept down her body, gently teasing it to life. He wanted this and so did Laura. He couldn't have begun to explain how good that made him feel!

David lay in bed, watching the sun painting patterns on the ceiling. He could hear water running as Laura took a shower. He closed his eyes, allowing himself the pleasure of simply remembering what had happened and how it had felt. 'Good' wasn't the word, 'great' was better, 'fantastic' wouldn't be going over-board!

He grinned as he threw his arm across his eyes to blot out the light while he mentally savoured each sweet caress, each kiss, all that raw potent passion they'd set alight in each other. He wouldn't have been human if he hadn't found himself comparing Laura to Kate at first, wondering if this caress or that way of kissing pleased her as well. But it had taken only a short while before all thoughts of another woman had disappeared from his head.

It was Laura he was making love to, and there had been no doubt of that in his mind. It had been her he'd wanted—for herself and not as a substitute—and yet the realisation allowed the first trickle of doubt to creep into his mind.

Should he have felt like that? Was it right to have put Kate out of his thoughts so easily?

'Bathroom's free.' Laura came into the room in a drift of spicy soap and steam, the bath towel she'd wrapped around herself covering her from breast to knee.

David felt his body jolt in immediate response and felt even worse. He tossed back the bedclothes, although it took him all his time to get out of bed, knowing that he was naked to Laura's gaze.

'David?' There was a question in her voice that made him stop, and he took a deep breath as he turned. He may have made a mistake but it wasn't fair to take it out on Laura. She had given herself to him with warmth and tenderness and an unstinting generosity. If he was wondering now if it had been right then it wasn't her fault but his. And because of that she deserved nothing less than the truth, hard though that might be.

'I'm sorry, Laura. I think it just hit me what happened.' It was difficult to explain yet so easy to feel the pain that scored his heart as he saw her smile fade. She turned away, holding the towel tightly around her as she went to pick up her clothes from beside the bed.

'I understand, David. I—I'll just go and get dressed, if you'll excuse me.'

So polite, so formal, so…so hurt! David stopped her as she made her way towards the door. This was his fault and he had to try to make up for what he'd done.

'Look, Laura, I—'

'Don't!' There was a flash of anger in her blue eyes as they soared to his. 'Don't you dare apologise, David Ross, or…or I shall do something drastic!'

'I wasn't going to apologise.' His tone was flat and he saw Laura blink as though the words had startled her. His fingers loosely encircled her wrist although there was no longer any need to hold her. Laura was waiting to hear what he had to say and how he prayed that he could come up with something which would help her understand the turmoil he felt.

'I'm not sorry about what happened just now. How could I be when it was so wonderful?' He smiled, watching the rapid play of emotions that crossed her face. The scent of her damp skin filled his nostrils, so enticing that his insides twisted with longing once again. But he had no intention of making this worse by giving into his desire a second time.

'But you do regret it?' Her voice was husky, telling him more about how she was feeling than the actual words could ever have done. She gave an empty laugh. 'It's possible to regret things and not feel sorry, David, so I do understand.' Her gaze went fleetingly to the photo on the bedside table before she smiled gently. 'It must be hard to let go. Perhaps it's impossible, but will you answer me just one question?'

'If I can.'

'Was it me you made love to just now or was it Kate?'

There was such yearning in her voice that David's heart seemed to break. He drew her to him, burying his face in her soft, damp hair and holding her as close as he could. 'You, Laura—only you!'

He heard the tiny sigh she gave before she slowly drew away from him. Raising her hand, she touched him lightly on the cheek. 'You know where I am if you want me, David.'

She left the room without another word but, then, what needed to be said after that? David sat on the bed and put his head in his hands. He felt close to despair, almost overwhelmed by a need to go after her, but then what? What could he offer her in exchange for what she was giving him? Until he could offer her his heart, proudly and without regret, there wasn't anything worthy of her.

The weekend crept past after Laura left. David set about filling the empty hours by gardening and shopping—doing all the hundred and one jobs he'd been putting off for months. He didn't see Laura at all so he had no idea if she was busy working in the house or had gone back to town.

By the time Sunday lunchtime arrived he'd done everything he could think of, and in a fit of desperation he rang his mother-in-law and arranged to collect the children himself rather than have her drive them back.

It was far too early when he arrived in Kendal so he veered off towards the hospital, assuring himself that it was his duty to check on how Elsie Chadwick was doing. After all, she was a visitor to the area and he had been called to attend to her.

Reasons ran thick and fast through his head but not one of them held a grain of truth until he arrived at the ward and discovered her friend, sitting on a hard plastic chair outside the doors. Hilda Dale's pleasure and relief at seeing a familiar face made him feel like a hypocrite, but at least it gave him something to concentrate on other than his own problems.

'Dr Ross... Oh, it is good of you to come all this way to see Elsie!' The elderly lady rose to her feet in a flurry of woolly jumpers and tweed. David took her cold hand and clasped it.

'How is Mrs Chadwick doing? Have the doctors said much?' he asked gently as they both sat down again.

'Yes and no.' Hilda Dale sighed. 'I didn't really understand half of what they said, to tell the truth, and I didn't like to ask because they seem so busy all the time. They said that Elsie had had a cerebral embolism. What is that, Dr Ross? I thought she'd had a stroke.'

'She has. To explain it simply, a cerebral embolism is a small blood clot which has found its way into an artery in the brain and interrupted the blood supply. Strokes can be caused by a cerebral embolism, as in Mrs Chadwick's case, or a cerebral thrombosis, which is when a clot builds up on the wall of an artery inside the brain, or by a haemorrhage, which occurs when a small blood vessel ruptures. All three causes what we commonly term a stroke.'

'I see. So, in Elsie's case, what will they do now?'

Hilda Dale sounded a little happier now that she was starting to understand.

'I imagine they'll have started Mrs Chadwick on a course of drugs to break down the clot and any others which may have formed and which could present a danger. A small daily dose of aspirin is usually the best way and causes the least side-effects.'

'Aspirin? Well, I never!' Mrs Dale gasped.

'High blood pressure is often an underlying cause so they might want your friend to take tablets to control it.' David shrugged. 'It's hard to say what they'll prescribe as there's a wide range, but it could be a simple diuretic. After that, it will be a question of seeing how much damage has been done.'

'Will Elsie be able to walk and talk again?' Hilda's eyes filled. 'I couldn't bear to think of her being bed-ridden.'

David patted the elderly woman's hand. 'An awful lot can be done to help a stroke patient recover her speech and mobility. Obviously it's impossible to say how severely affected Mrs Chadwick has been at this stage, but on the whole people who have suffered a stroke can lead an active life again. It's really a question of giving them all the support they need.'

'I understand.' Hilda Dale squared her shoulders. She glanced round as a nurse popped her head round the door and quietly informed her that she could see Mrs Chadwick for a few minutes.

She got up and shook David's hand. 'Thank you for coming, Dr Ross, and for explaining everything to me. Elsie and I have known one another for over forty years, and if she needs help then I'm more than willing to give it. What are friends for except to be there in a time of crisis?'

   She gave David a last smile then hurried into the
ward. David sighed as he watched her disappear. She
was right, of course, because that was exactly what a
friend was for. It made him more mixed up than ever.
Laura had been there for him in his time of crisis but
it hadn't been simple friendship he'd felt for her, not
by a long chalk!

CHAPTER EIGHT

'I FEEL bad about coming to see you, Dr Ross. You must be fed up, hearing about my problems!' Cyril Rogerson managed a laugh but it was an effort, David could tell.

'My only concern is to get you well again, Cyril. If you're feeling ill then you must come and see me. That's what I'm here for.' David sat back in his chair. It was Tuesday morning and surgery was almost over. Cyril had turned up without an appointment but David had had no hesitation about seeing him when Eileen had rung through. This needed getting to the bottom of, he thought as he saw how worn-out Cyril looked.

'I went into work this morning same as always, but I felt dreadful by eleven o'clock. It was the boss who told me to go home so I must have looked bad as he isn't one to worry unduly!' Cyril explained wryly.

'Well, I have to say that you don't look the picture of health, Cyril.' David got up and went around the desk. 'I'd just like to take a look at your gums, if you'd open your mouth.'

'Gums?' Cyril sounded bewildered but did as requested. David made a thorough check but he could find no trace of a blue-black line along Cyril's gums, which might have led to the conclusion that it was lead poisoning causing all the trouble, as Laura had suggested.

His heart gave a small leap at the thought of her, but he gave no outward sign of it as he picked up Cyril's notes. He hadn't seen or spoken to Laura since she'd left his house on Saturday morning. There had been no sign of her for the past two days so he could only assume that she'd gone back to town. Would she be back this coming weekend? He wouldn't like to think that Laura might be too embarrassed to come back because of what had gone on between them.

His breath caught as he recalled what they'd shared. Laura had been right when she'd said that he'd kept his anger at Kate's death bottled up for the children's sake. However, he was honest enough to admit that what had happened after that outpouring hadn't been just a reaction to the release. He'd wanted Laura for herself, and he wouldn't lie about his feelings even though it wasn't easy to deal with them.

Cyril cleared his throat, making David realise that he was still waiting. 'I see that you came into surgery on Saturday for those blood tests. Dr Sinclair has made a note on your card.

'And he also did a urine test in case it was a metabolic inbalance, didn't he? I asked him to do that to see if it showed something like ketosis, which can be caused by diabetes mellitus. The symptoms are fairly consistent with what you've told me—nausea, vomiting, loss of appetite. However, the test was clear on that score so I'm confident that isn't the cause.'

'Yes, that's what Dr Sinclair told me. Do you think the blood tests will show anything, Dr Ross?' Cyril ran a hand over his thinning grey hair, the tremble in it more pronounced than ever.

'I'm hoping so, Cyril. I've run through a whole list of possible causes and yet nothing seems to fit.' David sighed. 'Let's go back to the beginning, shall we? You were perfectly fit until you went to your daughter's? Did it all start with that cough?'

'I'm not sure.' Cyril frowned. 'I mean, the cough seemed to clear up right enough. Of course, it was the start of the hay fever season so that always makes me feel a bit low at first. I suppose it must have been around that time but I'm not sure. Maybe Marie can remember.'

'See if she can, will you, Cyril? I know your daughter married a farmer so is it possible that you came into contact with any chemicals used on the farm while you were staying with her?'

'No.' Cyril shook his head emphatically. 'Her hubbie uses only organic fertilisers and pesticides. He's doing really well, too, as there's a lot of folk wary of all these chemicals nowadays. Brian supplies one of the big supermarket chains with organically grown produce and his business is booming.'

'Then that seems to rule out that idea. So, just let me check once again. You've not had any headaches or diarrhoea? No abdominal pain? No sign of bleeding when you vomit? No dizziness or blurred vision?' David sighed as Cyril shook his head at each question. 'It's a mystery. The only other cause I can come up with for unrelated sickness is pregnancy, and somehow I don't think it's that, Cyril!'

Cyril laughed out loud. 'I don't think so, Dr Ross! Although a time or two these past weeks I would have been pleased as punch if it had been. At least then I'd know what was wrong. It's starting to get me down and that's a fact. It hits harder when you're used to being fit as a flea.'

'Well, we'll have you back to that just as soon as we can. I'm going to prescribe an antiemetic drug to control the vomiting. You can't keep on losing weight like this. The blood test results usually take a week to ten days but I'll try to get them through sooner.' David wrote out a prescription and handed it over. 'However, if anything else happens, call me, Cyril. We need to get to the bottom of this.'

'I will. Thanks, Dr Ross. You never know, maybe these will do the trick, eh?'

Cyril left and David sighed as he got up to take the morning's paperwork through for filing. There was something he was missing here. If only he could put his finger on what it was.

'Oh, there you are, David. I was hoping to catch you.'

He glanced round as he heard Elizabeth's voice. 'Did you want me for something?'

'There's no need to look so wary!' Elizabeth laughed as she came along the corridor to join him. 'It isn't a problem I'm about to burden you with but an invitation…to dinner with James and me tonight. I've invited Abbie and Sam as well.'

'What are we celebrating?'

'Nothing! I just thought it would be nice for us to get together, that's all. And Mrs Lewis keeps throwing out hints,' she added, referring to the elderly house-keeper who'd looked after her family for years. 'You know how she loves cooking for people, and I'm hardly ever in at the moment. I think she's getting with-drawal symptoms!'

'I can imagine.' David grinned. 'Mmm, doesn't seem all that long since I had that last invitation to your house—a rather *reluctant* invitation, if I remem-ber correctly.'

'You mean to that welcoming party for James? Although perhaps welcoming him wasn't quite what I had in mind,' Elizabeth admitted with a rueful smile. 'How things change!'

David laughed. 'Don't they just? Anyway, thanks, Liz. I'll see what I can do, although I'm not sure if Mike will be able to babysit. Still, I can always ask Trisha Shepherd to come round if he can't. She used to babysit quite a bit at one time.'

'Good idea. She'll probably be glad to get out of the house. Jeannie Shepherd was only saying the other day when I met her in town that old Isaac is driving them all mad now he's on the road to recovery after his heart attack. Seems he can't wait to get back to his farm. Harvey Walsh has been keeping an eye on things, but Isaac doesn't think Harvey's doing a very good job evidently.'

David laughed. 'Why doesn't that surprise me?'

Elizabeth hurried off after that. There was a list of home visits to attend to but David wasn't rostered for them. It was the weekly baby clinic that afternoon and it was his turn to attend. He grabbed a sandwich at the coffee-shop in the high street then walked back to the surgery, smiling as he found Sally Roberts, the local midwife, already setting up what they'd need for the afternoon.

'You're early,' he remarked, slipping his jacket over the back of a chair.

'Yes, I was already in the area so it seemed easier to come straight here than go on home.' Sally placed a paper sheet in the baby scales then gave David a considering look.

'What's that in aid of?' he asked curiously. 'Have I got a smut on my nose or something?'

'No. I was just wondering how much of what Marion

Rimmer told me was true and how much she'd made up to embroider the tale.'

David felt heat wash through him and turned away to take his stethoscope out of a drawer. 'Marion Rimmer has a tendency to embroider everything she says. Perhaps it would be better to bear that in mind.'

Sally obviously took the hint because she said nothing more. David concentrated on his work, trying not to think about the rumours that were circulating the town. They would die down as long as nothing more happened to fan their flames, he assured himself. Even as he thought of the havoc it had caused, he knew that Laura had been right. He might regret what had happened but he most certainly wasn't sorry about it!

'Right, that's fine. Ben is doing very well indeed, Lucy. He's making excellent progress.' David laughed as the five-month-old boy kicked his chubby little legs in the air as he lifted him out of the scales. He handed Ben to his mother, who promptly kissed the top of his downy head.

Lucy and her husband, John Fleming, had waited a long time for a child, undergoing a series of often uncomfortable tests and treatment. Lucy had been a teacher at the local infant school for many years, which must have heightened her distress at not having a child of her own. Baby Ben had been born thanks to the wonders of IVF treatment after ten years of marriage.

'He's such a good baby, too, Dr Ross. I can hardly believe my luck when I hear what some of the other mothers say about the sleepless nights they have. Ben sleeps right through now and has done for a while,' Lucy said proudly, slipping the baby into his cosy towelling jumpsuit and snapping the poppers shut.

'Obviously a very contented baby, Lucy. Sometimes you're just lucky and get one like that, and sometimes you get a child who absolutely refuses to settle at night.' David made a brief note on the baby's card. 'My own three are prime examples. Each one was different—' He broke off as there was a sudden scream from the waiting room. 'What on earth…?'

He was out of the room at a run, although he came to an abrupt halt as he took in the scene that met him. One of the young mums was sobbing hysterically as she watched Laura Mackenzie upending her baby, which was blue around the lips. As David watched, Laura gave the infant a sharp tap in the middle of its back and heard the spluttering gasp it gave as something shot from its mouth to land on the floor.

He went over to see what was going on, looking to Laura to explain rather than the terrified young woman. 'What happened?'

Laura smiled as she passed the baby back to its mum and bent to pick up a yellow pompon from the floor. 'Seems this young man took a fancy to the ties on his bonnet and decided to swallow one of them,' she explained, holding the soggy object out for his inspection.

'I see' David glanced at the young mother, who was cradling the screaming infant. 'It might be safer if you cut the pompons off, Paula. Babies are notorious for putting things into their mouths which shouldn't be there.'

'Oh, I will!' Paula shuddered. 'I wouldn't have known what to do if I'd been out in the street when it happened.' She turned to Laura with tears running in rivulets down her white face. 'I don't know how to thank you for what you just did!'

'That's all right. But if something like that ever happens again, don't panic. Turn your baby upside down and tap him sharply on the back to dislodge whatever he's swallowed. Nine times out of ten it will reappear, believe me!'

Sally came over, murmuring soothingly as she led Paula into the surgery. David watched them go then turned back to Laura, his heart skipping beats right and left as his eyes alighted on her beautiful face. He was overwhelmed by a need to reach out and touch her, but he couldn't do that when he knew that they were the object of all eyes.

'This is a surprise,' he said, as polite as a vicar at a tea party. 'I thought you'd gone back to town.'

'I did. I was on call on Sunday and at work yesterday. However, I had holidays owing so I decided to take them this week. It will give me time to get the sitting-room floor finished,' Laura explained in the same ultra-polite tone, but David could see a gleam of amusement in her eyes.

'I see.' He shot a glance over his shoulder then quickly led her from the waiting-room, closing the door behind them to stop anyone hearing their conversation. 'Did you want me for something urgent, then?'

'No. In fact, it wasn't you I was looking for.' Laura's smile took the sting out of the words, although David couldn't deny the disappointment he felt.

'Oh.' He glanced along the corridor as the telephone rang, but Eileen was in Reception and quickly answered it.

'I ran into Elizabeth in the high street and she invited me to dinner tonight. I forgot to ask her what time she wanted me there so I called in to check.' Laura's brows arched enquiringly. 'She said that you'd be there, too, David.'

'If I can manage to get a sitter for Emily.' His tone was a shade abrupt as he tried to get his head round the situation and how it made him feel. Knowing that Laura was going to be there tonight, it cast a different light on what would have been just a simple evening with colleagues.

Should he go now that he knew she'd be there, too? Or would it make the situation even more awkward than it already was? He was trying to decide when Laura touched his hand.

'If it would be easier for you, I could tell Elizabeth that I can't come tonight after all,' she suggested, locking into his thoughts with that ease which still surprised him. He had no idea how she did it but it made it impossible for him to make up excuses, as he might have been tempted to do.

'Do you think it's wise for us both to be there, Laura?'

'Do you mean, can we handle being in the same room? Yes, I think so.' She gave a gently mocking laugh, her blue eyes teasing him as she laid her hand on her heart. 'I promise on my honour that I won't give in to my lustful urges tonight, David, so you'll be quite safe!'

He found himself laughing, too. 'Thank you. That really sets my mind at rest! Actually, Liz is out on some calls at the moment. I can ask her to give you a ring when she gets back. I forgot to ask her what time she wanted me there so I'm not much help!' He sobered suddenly. 'I'm afraid the rumours have started. Marion Rimmer obviously lost no time in letting it be known you stayed at my house on Friday night.'

'I'm sure we can deal with them.' There was a sudden tightness to her voice and she gave him a brilliant yet empty smile. 'I'd better be off. If you'd ask Elizabeth to ring me...'

'I'm sorry to bother you, David, but I've got Annie Jackson on the phone. She's in a bit of a state so could you come and speak to her?' Eileen popped her head out of the office just at that moment.

'Is it young Sean?' he asked, as he hurried along the corridor.

'No, something about Chloe, but I can't make head or tail of what she is saying,' Eileen replied, stepping aside so that he could pass her.

David picked up the phone, aware that Laura had followed him and was standing just inside the doorway. 'Hello, Annie, it's Dr Ross here. Tell me what's wrong.' He listened carefully but it wasn't easy to follow what Annie was saying because she was so upset. 'What was that? Chloe has a rash?' He glanced round as Laura touched his arm, miming that she'd like to speak to Annie. 'Annie, Dr Mackenzie is here with me at the moment. She'd like a word with you. Hold on.'

He passed the receiver over to Laura, waiting while she spoke quietly to Chloe's mother. She looked worried when she hung up. 'Annie says that Chloe is covered in a bright red rash all over her arms and face.'

'Oh, dear. That isn't good news, is it?' David said softly.

'It isn't. It could be a sign that her body's rejecting the transplanted bone marrow.' Laura sighed. 'She's done so well up till now, too. The tests we ran last week were very encouraging, but graft-versus-host disease can crop up at any time.'

'Actually, I thought she was still in hospital,' David said. 'Because of Sean having mumps.'

'It wasn't possible to keep her in any longer when,

to all intents, she was perfectly fit. We needed the room she was in,' Laura explained. 'Annie was finding it hard to cope, looking after Sean and getting to the hospital each day, so her mother offered to have him to stay. The other two boys have been vaccinated so, with Sean out of the house, the risk to Chloe was negligible and she went home yesterday. But this is very worrying. Would you mind very much if I went with you to see her, David? She'll need re-admitting immediately if it is GVHD.'

'Of course I don't mind. Just give me ten minutes or so to clear up here and I'll drive you over to the Jacksons',' he assured her.

Annie Jackson looked as though she'd aged a good ten years when she opened the door to them less than half an hour later. 'Oh, I'm so glad you came. I didn't know what to do...'

David patted her arm. 'You did exactly the right thing, Annie. Now, let's have a look at Chloe and see what's wrong with her.'

Annie quickly led the way along the narrow hall to the living-room and opened the door. Chloe was sitting on the battered sofa, playing with a doll. She looked up when the door opened and her face lit up when she saw Laura.

'Dr Laura!' she exclaimed in delight, getting up and running over to greet her. She didn't appear to be at all ill, which surprised David.

'Hello, Chloe. How are you?' Laura took the little girl's hand and led her back to the sofa. She turned Chloe's face towards the light and studied the rash that peppered her cheeks. Then she checked the child's arms, bending closer to examine the bright red spots.

She turned to David and he was surprised to see

amusement on her face. 'Can you come and take a look at this very interesting rash, Dr Ross, and see what you think about it?'

David frowned as he crossed the room, wondering what had amused her. He bent and studied the rash, then had to bite his lip to stop himself laughing. 'Mmm, I see what you mean, Dr Mackenzie,' he said solemnly. 'At a guess, I'd say it was a case of feltus crayonus—would you agree?'

'Oh, I think that's a fairly accurate diagnosis, Dr Ross. But perhaps we should perform a little test just to be certain.' Laura was finding it hard not to laugh as she turned to Annie. 'Have you got a damp flannel, Annie?'

'Why, yes, of course.' Annie looked perplexed but she hurried from the room and returned a few seconds later with a facecloth.

'Thank you. Now, take a look at this.' Laura gently wiped the wet cloth over Chloe's cheek then held it out for Annie's inspection.

'Why it's covered in red...' Annie gasped as she looked at her daughter's cheek and saw that the rash had disappeared.

'What did you use to make the spots, Chloe?' David asked gently 'Was it a felt-tipped crayon?'

Chloe nodded, staring down at the doll she was holding. Annie sat down on a chair as her legs threatened to give way. 'I can't believe she did that. Or that I was taken in...' She flushed. 'I feel such a fool, Dr Ross, getting you and Dr Mackenzie out here. I just panicked when I saw the spots and ran to the phone!'

'Don't you worry about it, Annie.' David laughed as he tilted Chloe's face. 'Why did you do it, sweetheart? You gave your mummy a real fright, you know.'

'Charlie told me to,' Chloe mumbled, twisting the hem of the doll's gaudy red and yellow dress around her finger.

'Charlie?' David queried, glancing at Annie, but it was Laura who explained.

'Charlie's in the same ward as Chloe was in. He's her friend. Isn't that right, poppet?'

Chloe nodded. Her hair was just starting to grow back, the downy brown fuzz catching the light from the window. 'He's my best friend,' she muttered, 'and it's his birthday tomorrow.'

'Ah-h, I see!' Laura grinned at David. 'Whenever any of the children on the ward have a birthday we hold a party for them. Did you want to go to Charlie's party, Chloe? Is that why you gave yourself this rash?'

'Uh-huh.' Chloe slid her thumb into her mouth, watching them with wary brown eyes. She took her thumb out again with a popping noise when she saw that they didn't look angry. 'Charlie said that you'd send me back to hospital if I was sick. Then I'd be able to go to his party.' She turned to David, obviously wanting him to understand how important it was. 'There'll be jelly and cakes and a conjie…conjie man.'

'A conjurer, who does magic tricks?' David laughed softly as he stood up. 'Well, I can see why you'd want to go to such a super party, Chloe. Maybe Dr Laura can arrange it for you.'

He glanced at Laura for confirmation. She smiled as she stood up. 'Oh, I think I can sort something out. But you have to promise not to give your mummy a fright again. OK?'

Chloe nodded, obviously thrilled that she'd be going to the party even though her ruse had failed. Annie led the way down the hall and opened the door.

'I can't believe she did that. One of the boys, yes, but Chloe...'

David laughed. 'Kids never fail to surprise you!'

'And look on it as a good sign,' Laura added. 'Sick children rarely cause mischief. Obviously, Chloe is on the mend.'

They left the Jacksons' house and David drove back to the surgery. He parked the car then turned as Laura spoke.

'Children are so astute, aren't they, David? They soon sum up a situation.'

'You mean Chloe?' he queried, even though he sensed a deeper meaning to the remark.

'Yes. Obviously, she or Charlie must have overheard somebody discussing what to look out for after a bone-marrow transplant and that's why they latched onto the idea of her having a rash.' Laura paused before she continued quietly, 'I wouldn't want your children to be hurt by the rumours that are going round town, David. I care too much about you all to want that to happen.'

'I know you do.' He touched her hand, almost over-whelmed by her consideration. 'I'm sure that the gossip will die down pretty quickly once there's something else for folk to talk about.'

'Let's hope so.' She got out of the car, waiting until David had got out as well. 'If you could ask Elizabeth to ring me, I'd appreciate it. Maybe I'll see you tonight, then.'

She made her way down the drive and turned out of the gates. David sighed as he went inside the building. This situation was difficult for both of them, yet it wasn't only the gossip that was causing the problem. If only he could look to the future, and not keep think-ing about the past, it would be so much easier to know what to do. But it would be out of the question to do that. He couldn't live with himself if he forgot about Kate.

'Daddy, is Laura going to be our new mummy?'

Emily's clear little voice rang around the kitchen, stopping David in his tracks. He carefully put the hot grill pan on a trivet before he turned.

'What makes you ask that, darling?'

Emily gave him a beautiful innocent smile as she speared a piece of sausage with her fork. 'Kelly said that Peter used to stay the night at her house and sleep in her mummy's bed before he became her new daddy. She told me that was why Laura had stayed here with you.'

Emily popped the chunk of sausage into her mouth and chewed it in expectant silence as she waited for an answer. David tried his best to think one up but it wasn't easy. He shot a glance at Mike but his son steadfastly refused to return his gaze as he stared fixedly at his plate.

David took a deep breath, not sure where to begin. 'Laura did stay here on Friday night. She slept in your room, Emily, in fact. All the lights went out in her house and she didn't want to stay there on her own in the dark.'

Emily nodded, readily accepting the explanation as it made so much sense. 'Did Peebody stay here as well?'

'Yes. He's afraid of the dark, would you believe? He has to have a night-light on, and when he slept here in the kitchen I had to leave a light on for him as well.'

Emily laughed out loud at the idea of the huge dog

being frightened. 'Isn't he silly? Everyone knows that there's nothing to be scared of, is there, Daddy?'

'Of course not, poppet.' David gave her a hug and mentally crossed his fingers, but it seemed that Emily hadn't been sidetracked, as he'd hoped.

'So is Laura going to be our new mummy, then? I hope she is. I like Laura. She lets me paint and she doesn't mind if I make a mess. And she bakes brilliant cakes!' Emily turned huge dark eyes on David. 'You do like Laura, don't you, Daddy?'

'I… Well, yes, of course I do,' David floundered as he searched for the right words, but was there any such thing as a right way of handling a situation like this?

'That's what I told Kelly!' Emily popped the last bite of sausage into her mouth and swallowed it hurriedly. 'Can I get down, please?'

Emily hurried from the kitchen when David nodded, although for a moment he wished he'd tried harder to make her understand the situation. He glanced at Mike as he pushed back his chair and carried his plate over to the sink, realising that he had to say something about what had gone on.

'Look, Mike, I don't want you getting the wrong idea about Friday—' he began,

'Chill out, Dad. Laura stayed the night—so what? It's no big deal.' Mike shrugged as he slid his plate into the bowl of soapy water. He ran his hands down his jeans to dry them then headed for the door. 'I'm going over to Danny's. He's going to help me with this media studies assignment. See you later.'

Mike was gone before David could get another word out. He sighed. He'd handled that really well, hadn't he?

*　　*　　*

'Red or white, David?'

James held two bottles of wine aloft and David forced himself to smile. 'Oh, red, I think. Thanks.'

He accepted the glass and sat down on the sofa, listening to the hum of voices. Abbie and Sam were talking to Elizabeth but he didn't try to join in the conversation. He wasn't sure any contributions he made would make much sense.

The door opened and he jumped even though he hadn't heard the bell ringing, but it was only Mrs Lewis, coming to check if they had everything they needed. David took a sip of his wine, hoping it would steady his nerves as he waited for Laura to arrive. He felt like a boy on his first date, which was ridiculous in view of what had happened a couple of days before.

The bell rang and a few drops of wine slopped out of his glass. He set it down on a coaster then took his handkerchief out of his pocket to mop up the spill. He could hear laughter coming from the hall and immediately recognised Laura's husky tones.

He rose to his feet as she came into the room, feeling his head swirl as he saw how beautiful she looked that night in a pale pink dress which enhanced her very feminine curves. She was even wearing high heels— elegant cream leather sandals which added a couple of inches to her height yet somehow only seemed to emphasise how tiny she was as she came over to greet him.

'So you made it, then,' she said softly, her eyes lifting to his.

'Yes.' He had to clear his throat. 'I managed to get a sitter for Emily.'

'Good.' She gave him a cool little smile then turned

to go over to where Abbie and Sam were standing, laughing at something Sam said to her.

David's hand tightened on his glass as he was overcome by a sudden surge of jealousy which shocked him. He didn't own Laura! But, no matter how foolish it was, he couldn't deny that he hated to see her responding to another man that way.

'I must say that it's good to have time together away from work,' James came over to join him and David struggled to get his emotions in check.

'It is. How are the plans for the wedding progressing? Is it all sorted out now?' he asked, barely listening as James launched into an amusing anecdote about the trials and tribulations involved in finalising the arrangements. His attention was firmly focused on Laura, although he couldn't hear what she was saying—

'David?'

He came back to earth with a jolt, to find James watching him with an amused smile on his mouth. 'Sorry, what was that? I didn't catch it.'

'Hmm, so I gathered,' James said dryly. He turned as Elizabeth came to join them, slipping his arm round her shoulders in a gesture which spoke volumes about his feelings for her. 'I was just telling David that we were wondering if Emily would like to be one of our bridesmaids.'

'Oh, good. I've been meaning to ask you for a while now, but never seemed to get the chance.' Elizabeth brushed James's cheek with an affectionate kiss. 'It was James's idea and I do hope you'll agree. We'd love to have Emily as a bridesmaid if she'd like to be one. Do you think she would?'

'I'm sure she'd be thrilled.' David smiled, warmed

by his friends' generosity. 'Wait until I tell her. She'll be over the moon!'

'Who will? What am I missing?' Laura asked, coming over to join them. David felt a small thrill run through him as her shoulder brushed his arm as she stopped beside him. The contact was so brief that it shouldn't have caused him the least bother, but he could barely breathe let alone answer the question. It was left to Elizabeth to explain, which she did.

'We were just asking David if Emily could be a bridesmaid at our wedding. We were thinking of asking little Chloe Jackson as well.'

'What a lovely idea!' Laura's voice was full of warmth, her blue eyes sparkling as she turned to David. 'You will let Emily do it, won't you?'

'Of course.' He frowned, wondering why Laura should have imagined that he might refuse. Abbie claimed Elizabeth's attention just then, and she and James moved away to speak to her, leaving him and Laura alone.

'Why do I get the impression that you thought I might not agree to Emily being a bridesmaid?'

Laura shrugged as she sipped her wine. Her blue eyes were very clear as they met his over the rim of the glass. 'I just got the impression the other day that you don't like the children getting too heavily involved with other people.'

David could feel a nerve begin to twitch in his jaw. He looked down at his glass, not wanting her to see how that statement made him feel. If he'd tried to discourage Emily's growing attachment to Laura it was because he hadn't been able to handle how *he'd* felt. And nothing had changed in that respect.

'I do understand, David.' Laura touched his arm.

David's eyes flew to her face and became locked there, held by the expression in her eyes—all that warmth and concern, that tender understanding and love.

His heart started beating so fast that he felt he could barely stand. Laura loved him? Was it possible? Or was he simply seeing things he wanted to see? Yet how much sense did that make? Surely the last thing he wanted was for Laura to fall in love with him when it would cause such upheaval in both their lives.

He was so mixed up that it took him several seconds before he could reply. 'Do you?'

'Yes. You're afraid of the children being hurt and are naturally very protective of them. But children are far more resilient than we give them credit for.'

Mercifully, he was saved from having to answer as Mrs Lewis appeared just then to tell them that dinner was ready. Elizabeth led the way to the dining-room, where the table had been laid with the best china and crystal. Once everyone was seated Mrs Lewis happily set about serving the meal, obviously in her element at having so many people to fuss over.

'There now, there's plenty more soup in the tureen so help yourselves.' The elderly housekeeper smiled in satisfaction as she heard the appreciative murmurs they all made as they tasted the delicious cream of asparagus soup she'd prepared. 'There's lamb and mint sauce next and one of my sherry trifles for afters so make sure you leave plenty of room for it.'

'Thank you, Mrs Lewis, it all looks—and tastes— wonderful.' Elizabeth smiled as Mrs Lewis left the room. 'Right, tuck in, everyone. Knowing Mrs Lewis, there'll be enough food to feed an army and we have to do it justice!'

Conversation flowed along general channels over

dinner. Laura had everyone laughing as she regaled them with the tale of what Chloe had done. Mrs Lewis had placed candles in the centre of the table and Laura's animated face looked even more exquisite in the glow they cast.

She had pinned her hair into a loose knot on top of her head, which showed off the elegant length of her neck and the delicate curves of her ears. She was wearing tiny diamond studs in her lobes and they winked and glinted as they caught the candlelight.

David drank in the picture she made, so beautiful and desirable that he wouldn't have been a man if he hadn't been aware of it. His eyes moved to Sam as the younger man claimed Laura's attention, darkening as she laughed at something Sam said.

Was Laura attracted to Sam? The young doctor had quite a reputation in the town, although Sam and Abbie seemed to spend a lot of their time together. But if Sam imagined that he could toy with Laura's feelings…

As *he* was toying with them? the pesky voice of his conscience whispered. Surely, if anyone at this table was being unfair to Laura then it was him. Hadn't he just seen how she'd looked at him? How much more proof did he need of her feelings? And what was he going to do about it?

'What do you think, David—?' Abbie broke off as the phone suddenly rang shrilly in the hall, mercifully sparing him of the embarrassment of admitting that he hadn't been listening. Conversation came to an abrupt halt as they heard Mrs Lewis going to answer it, then the sound of her footsteps coming towards the dining room. Nobody was surprised when she popped her head round the door with a message for Sam, who was on call that night.'

'It's the mountain rescue people, Dr O'Neill. Can they have a word with you, please? It's urgent.'

'Typical!' Sam looked regretfully at the dish of sherry trifle as he stood up. 'I'm sure folk *know* when you're in the middle of a meal!'

He hurried into the hall and they could hear him talking on the phone. He was back within minutes, his expression very grim. 'There's been an accident—a bad one, too, by the sound of it. A group of climbers has had a fall over at the Chimney. At least three are injured, one very badly. I'm going over there now to see what I can do.'

'I'd better come with you,' David offered immediately, standing up.

'Me, too. With that many injured it's going to take all of us to deal with the casualties.' James got up as well. He smiled ruefully at Elizabeth. 'Looks like our dinner party has come to an abrupt end!'

'Oh, I don't know.' Elizabeth laughed as she glanced at the other two women. '*We* can still enjoy ourselves while you three go haring off over the mountains. Have fun, boys!'

It took only a few minutes for everyone to get sorted out. Sam would drive them there as he'd come in his car in case he got called out. They'd need to stop off for suitable clothing *en route* as going up into the mountains without them was foolhardy in the extreme.

David went to follow Sam out to the car then stopped when Laura called to him. She followed him out to the steps, standing on the top one so that she was almost at his eye level for once. 'Would you like me to keep an eye on Emily until Mike gets back?'

'Could you?' David frowned. 'I don't know how long this is going to take, and I don't want to keep

Trisha hanging about. Mike shouldn't be late, though, so if you could tell him what's happened I'd be grateful.'

'Don't worry. I'll sort things out.' Laura made a small involuntary move towards him then stopped abruptly. 'Take care, David'

'I will.' His eyes held hers for a moment which seemed to last for an eternity before he turned and ran down the steps. He got into the car, slamming the door, then Sam headed down the drive. David closed his eyes, letting himself savour that last moment when Laura had looked at him…

He felt his heart ache with a searing pain. Laura had wanted to kiss him just now. It was only the fact that the others were watching that had stopped her. Was he being fair to either of them by letting this continue? Yet what was the alternative? Never to see her again? No matter how much guilt he felt, that thought was infinitely worse!

CHAPTER NINE

'LONGITUDINAL compression of the spine, without a doubt. He must have fallen at least twenty feet straight down.'

David glanced up from where he was kneeling next to the injured climber. 'I can feel definite signs of swelling in the centre of his lower back and it's obvious he's in a great deal of pain. There might be internal injuries as well but I daren't risk moving him to check. They'll be picked up when he's X-rayed.'

'What are we going to do, David? It's going to be no joke getting him out of here, especially with a back injury!' Mark Winters, leader of the mountain rescue team, sounded worried, as well he might.

'I can see that.' David sighed as he looked around. The accident couldn't have happened in a worse place. The climber had fallen into what was known locally as the Chimney, a gaping fissure in the rock.

It would be a difficult climb out of there for an able-bodied person, using all the right equipment, and near impossible to recover a stretcher with a badly injured man strapped to it. The most important thing at present was to ensure that the climber wasn't jolted about otherwise he could end up paralysed.

David turned back to the young man as he groaned. He looked to be in his early twenties, his hands and face bearing dozens of cuts and bruises from where he'd slithered down the rock-face. However, those injuries were superficial. It was the damage to his spine that was the real cause for concern.

'How are you doing there, Andy?'

'Not so good, Doc. I—' Andy gasped, sweat beading his forehead at the pain it caused when he moved unwittingly.

'Lie still! Whatever you do, you mustn't move,' David ordered. He turned to Mark. 'Can you shine that torch over here? I'm going to give him a shot for the pain.'

Mark directed the beam of the torch while David administered an injection of morphine. David checked the patient's pulse again, frowning as he felt how rapid it was. Andy's skin was very cool as well so he ripped open one of the packs of foil blankets, which the mountain rescue team always carried, and tucked it around the young man.

It was obvious that Andy was in shock and David would have liked to set up a drip, but it wasn't feasible when his main concern had to be to get the injured man out of there as fast as possible.

'We need to get him to hospital as soon as we can,' he said in a low voice as he stood up. 'He doesn't have a chance unless he gets specialised treatment urgently.' He looked up towards the top of the fissure, where lights had been rigged up, and grimaced. 'It's going to be one hell of a job getting him out of here, though.'

'I know.' Mark's tone was grim as he also cast a glance up the sheer rock-face. 'I'm going to go up top and see what's happening up there. Then we'll decide what we're going to do about this young fellow. It's a damn good job the three of you came tonight otherwise I don't know how we'd have coped. The place looked like a war zone, with bodies lying about everywhere, when we got here. People should have more sense.'

David silently agreed as he watched Mark climb expertly out of the narrow funnel. From what he'd gathered from the uninjured members of the party, they were from a climbing club in the Midlands and of mixed abilities. Whose decision it had been to attempt the Chimney he had no idea, but Mark and his colleagues had left everyone in little doubt of their view that the group had been lucky to get off as lightly as they had.

Two had broken ankles and another a fractured pelvis. Andy had fared the worst, crashing feet first right to the bottom of the drop. David knew that to get him out without causing permanent damage to his spinal cord was going to be one of the hardest tasks he'd ever undertaken.

'Right, everything seems to be sorted out up there.' Mark came down the Chimney again, making the climb look easy because he knew what he was doing. 'Some of my lot are going to get the rest of the injured down to the road. The ambulance is already there, waiting. Sam and James are going with them.'

'Good. As for this one, well, I think the only solution is to get the helicopter out here,' David decided. 'If they can lower a cable and take the stretcher out flat, it will be far better than dragging it up lengthways. I don't want to risk any pressure being put on Andy's spine.'

'Makes sense to me. Let's go for it.' Mark switched on his radio, briefly informing one of his colleagues to contact the RAF search and rescue squad. A cradle stretcher was lowered into the Chimney as it would provide the best support for the injured man when he was moved. However, getting him onto it was a tricky manoeuvre in itself.

It took David and Mark, as well as another of the rescue team, to transfer him onto it. David fitted the young man with a cervical collar first and strapped his legs together to prevent any undue movement. Then, with a great deal of care, they managed to slide a spinal board beneath him, but David didn't breathe easily until Andy was lying in the cradle. Using an inflatable head support, he secured the young man's head. Once he was happy that he'd done everything possible to minimise any movement, David covered the young climber with another blanket, strapped him in then settled down to wait for the helicopter to arrive.

It didn't take long before they heard the beat of the helicopter's rotors overhead. Then the real fun began. David checked his patient's vital signs one last time, then quietly explained what he wanted him to do. 'I want you to remain as still as possible. I know it's going to be hard but, believe me, Andy, it's vital you do that. How's the pain? Do you need another shot?'

'No...' Andy bit his lip, struggling to hold back the tears. 'Will I be paralysed, Doc?'

'We're doing everything we can to avoid that happening.' David laid his hand briefly on the young man's shoulder. 'Good luck, now.'

It was a heart-stopping operation. It was easy enough to lower the cable into the Chimney, but holding the helicopter steady overhead so that the cradle didn't bang against the walls was a Herculean task.

Inch by inch the stretcher rose, with Mark and the other man climbing alongside it. Each man clung to the rock-face with one hand, using the other to stop the cradle swinging into the rock-face. David's heart was in his mouth as he watched from below. All it would take was one tiny jolt to the left or right...

The cradle cleared the rim of the Chimney and a huge cheer went up as it disappeared into the belly of the big yellow helicopter. It disappeared into the night, taking Andy to the spinal unit at Stoke. Only then did David breathe a sigh of relief. At least the young fellow had a chance.

The rescue team hauled David out of the Chimney, using the complex arrangement of ropes and pulley they'd set up. David knew that he wouldn't have had a hope of making the climb either up or down if it hadn't been for that. As it was, his legs were trembling when he was finally back on top, but even that wasn't the end of it. There was still a long walk back along the sheep path to the road where the vehicles were parked.

He was exhausted when he got there, longing for a hot bath and bed. He looked round, wondering what had happened to Sam and James. Had they gone with the ambulance to the hospital?

His gaze skimmed along the line of vehicles parked beside the road, and he felt his heart stop for a moment as his gaze alighted on a familiar khaki-rust Land Rover. His legs seemed to be made from jelly as he made his way towards it, although whether it was fatigue which was causing the reaction or disbelief he wasn't sure.

Laura leaned over and opened the door for him, her face just a pale oval in the dashboard light. 'Want a lift?'

David glanced round, wondering if he was dreaming. Mark gave him a wave then climbed into one of the trucks. Most of the rescue team had left already, eager to get home to their beds. Mark reversed down the road until he was level with David and stuck his head out of the window.

'Thanks for tonight, David—a real team effort, I'd call it.' He glanced at Laura and grinned. 'Well, I won't keep you, then.'

Mark was gone in a second, the last remaining truck following close behind. David waited until their rear lights were just pinpricks before he slowly climbed into the Land Rover and closed the door.

'I'm sorry. I shouldn't have come, should I?' There was a world of pain in Laura's voice as she prepared to put the vehicle into gear. David's hand closed around hers, then he lifted it to his lips and kissed her small fingers. His voice was hoarse with emotion but suddenly he couldn't pretend any more.

'I can't think of anything I wanted more than to see you there, waiting for me.'

She gave him a brilliant smile, her fingers resting against his lips for a moment before she gently withdrew her hand. They didn't say anything at all on the drive back to Yewdale, but words would have been superfluous. David rested his head against the seat as they drove and let his mind go blank. He didn't want to think about anything apart from what was happening at that moment. There would be time enough to worry about other things later.

'Come in. I'll make some coffee. You must be dying for a cup.'

Laura led the way into her house through the kitchen, switching on lights as she went. David followed her inside but he didn't get very far. His eyes widened with appreciation as he came to a halt and looked around. Laura hadn't been kidding when she'd hinted at how hard she'd been working. He could hardly believe the changes she'd made in such a short space of time.

'Like it?' Laura came back to see what was keeping him, smiling as she saw the expression on his face. 'They're the original cupboards. It just goes to show what you can do with a bit of paint.'

'It does.' David's eyes swept over the cupboards, which had been stripped of their old chipped varnish and stained a soft blue so that the grain of the wood showed through.

The ugly wallpaper he remembered had gone as well and the walls were now painted a sunny yellow with a row of vivid blue and purple pansies stencilled above the newly tiled splashback. White muslin curtains hung at the window, framing the view of the old apple tree.

There was a delicious smell of baking in the room, which added to its overall appeal. David's nose twitched appreciatively. Chocolate cake? His stomach growled. Definitely chocolate cake!

'Hungry?' Once again Laura homed in on his thoughts as she went to the dresser. Lifting a cover, she held out the cake for his inspection then laughed as she saw his expression. 'I don't think you need answer that! Go on through to the sitting-room while I cut you a slice.'

David shrugged off his jacket then grimaced as he saw his grimy hands. 'Do you mind if I wash first?'

'Of course not. Anyway, it'll give me time to get the coffee ready.' She nodded towards the door. 'Bathroom's upstairs, first door on your right. There's plenty of hot water so feel free to have a shower if you want one.'

'Thanks.' David had no intention of taking advantage of the offer, but once he was in the bathroom the thought of rinsing off the grime with hot water was too good to resist. He stripped quickly and stepped into the bath, smiling to himself as he saw the antiquated shower apparatus looped over the taps.

Laura was obviously doing one room at a time, and the claw-footed bath and unwieldly shower attachment were obviously originals! Still, the water was hot and there was a fresh bar of soap, whose perfume instantly brought Laura to mind as he lathered himself.

He felt his body surge to life and quickly rinsed off the suds, but he could still smell the scent clinging to his skin—Laura's scent, that softly subtle fragrance he would have recognised anywhere!

He stepped out of the bath and picked up a towel, seeing the lines of strain that bracketed his mouth as he caught a glimpse of himself in the mirror. Was that all it took, something as simple as using her soap, to make him feel this raw surge of desire? He didn't know how the realisation made him feel, wasn't sure he wanted to know even. It was bound up with too many other thoughts which were far too painful.

'David...coffee's ready.'

Laura tapped on the door and he took a deep breath, struggling to chase the unsettling thoughts from his head. 'I'll be right there.'

He made his way to the kitchen once he was dressed again but there was no sign of Laura. He backtracked along the hall and found her sitting in isolated splendour in the sitting-room. Apart from a huge, squashy sofa, the room was bare yet somehow still managed to look cosily inviting, the fire which was burning in the grate settling a soft glow everywhere. There was a row of thick creamy-white candles in pottery holders along the mantelpiece, the flickering light from them casting shadows on the ivory-painted walls. David was instantly struck by how peaceful the room seemed as he went in to join her.

She looked round as she heard his footsteps on the bare wooden floor, and grinned. 'Ah, there you are. Sorry about the lack of furniture but I haven't found what I want yet, apart from this sofa. I promised myself when I bought this place that everything I chose was going to be *exactly* what I wanted. None of this buying by the yard, so to speak.'

'By the yard?' David frowned as he sat down on the sofa. He took a mug of coffee from the tray on the floor between them. 'What do you mean by that?'

'Oh, you must have seen those magazines where they feature people's homes. You know what I mean, houses were everything is perfect—each cushion precisely placed, every single book the same height and colour.' Laura laughed as she curled her legs up beneath her. 'I used to wonder how on earth people found books that matched like that, and then I read this article, telling you where you could buy books *by the yard*! Evidently, they weren't meant to be *read*. They were to be used as an accessory like...like a vase of flowers or a potted plant. I swore that I would never, ever resort to that!'

'I don't blame you.' David laughed at the idea. He put down his cup and cast a wistful glance at the slice of cake. 'I hope that's for me.'

'Of course.' Laura bent to hand it to him at the same moment as David reached for the plate, and their hands touched. David felt the surge of awareness that raced through him and drew back abruptly. Laura handed him the plate without a word but both of them were aware of the tension that filled the room at that moment.

He dug a pastry fork into the cake while he struggled to keep a grip on his emotions, but it wasn't the easiest thing he'd ever had to do. Soft lights and a beautiful woman were hardly dampeners to a man's instincts, especially when that woman was Laura.

He swallowed a mouthful of the cake without really tasting it as he wondered if he should hurry up and leave. He wasn't a saint and being here like this was a test of his self-control he wasn't sure he'd win. It wasn't fair to Laura to allow anything to happen again when he was so confused about his feelings.

'I stayed with Emily until Mike got back. And I left Peebody with them. I hope that was all right. Mind you, I wouldn't like to say who was minding whom. The silly dog was looking decidedly nervous at the thought of being left here on his own!'

Laura laughed softly but there was a hint of strain in her voice of which he was immediately conscious. Was this as difficult for her as it was for him? he wondered before he could stop himself. It was hardly the most steadying of thoughts.

'Of course I don't mind. And they'll be company for each other, I imagine,' he replied thickly.

'Mmm, that's what I thought.' Laura plucked at a thread which had started to unravel from the cuff of her sweater. She was still wearing the pink dress but she'd slipped a chunky fisherman's knit pullover over it, David noted almost absently before such thoughts came to an abrupt stop as Laura continued quietly, 'Emily told me that she knew Peebody needed to have a night-light on and…and that you'd left one on for him when we stayed with you on Friday.'

David put his plate down on the tray with a click which sounded like an explosion to his over-stretched nerves. He'd heard the question in Laura's voice but he didn't know how to answer it. Should he tell her the whole story—what Emily had said to him at tea that night? Suddenly he wasn't sure if it would be wise but he had to say something to explain.

'One of Emily's schoolfriends mentioned about you staying on Friday night.' He shrugged, striving for a nonchalance he wished he felt. 'She must have heard her parents talking about it, I expect. That's the trouble with a town like this—everybody knows what goes on.'

'Then I'm sorry I put you in such a difficult position.' Laura got up abruptly. She went to the fire and poked the coals viciously so that flames shot up the chimney. She turned round and glared at him, her very stance a challenge. 'As I told you earlier, I didn't mean to make things awkward for you, David!'

'I know you didn't!' He felt suddenly angry, though whether with her or himself or just this whole confusing situation he wasn't sure. He stood up as well and his face was set in the flickering firelight. 'Neither of us planned what happened on Friday night.'

'Do you think *I* don't know that?' She gave a harsh laugh. Her blue eyes sparkled with anger as they clashed with his. 'As I also know how much you regret it happening. You've made that very plain. But don't worry, David, because there won't be a repeat. I know how you feel, believe me! Now, I think it would be better if we said goodnight, don't you? I'd hate for there to be any more rumours circulating about our *goings-on*!'

'For heaven's sake!' David wasn't even aware of moving, but suddenly he had hold of Laura by the shoulders. He gave her a quick shake, his anger moving up another notch as she glared at him.

'For heaven's sake what? Don't you think I should feel angry because you're ashamed of what we did?' she spat at him, like a small cat backed into a corner.

'Ashamed?' David could barely believe what he was hearing. He gave her another quick shake so that her hair tumbled loose, silky curls falling around her face. 'Damn it, I'm not *ashamed* of making love to you, Laura!'

'Oh, no?' Her laughter was as brittle as glass, hard with disbelief. 'That wasn't the impression you gave me.'

'Then maybe it's you who's at fault, not me!' His eyes blazed into hers and he saw the first stirrings of uncertainty cross her face. His tone softened all of a sudden as the anger drained out of him as fast as it had come. 'If I gave you that impression then I apologise.'

'But you don't feel right about it, do you?' She managed a smile but her eyes were clouded as they met his. It was obvious that she wanted him to deny the accusation, but how could he when it was true?

David let her go abruptly, unable to look into her face and not do something both of them would only come to regret. Laura was hurt and bewildered by the way he was behaving and it broke his heart to see the evidence of it in her beautiful blue eyes. But he didn't dare run the risk of hurting her even more. At the end of the day, he might never be able to give Laura what she wanted from him, no matter that a part of him yearned to do so.

'I don't know how I feel, Laura, except that I'm not

ashamed of what happened between us.' He stared at the ceiling as he struggled to explain. 'I suppose, deep down, that I'm afraid that if I let myself love you then it's as though all the promises I made to Kate were lies. I...I don't know if I could live with myself, thinking that.'

'I understand, David.' Laura drew herself up but he could see the effort it cost her. 'I know how difficult this is for you and I don't want to make it worse. Maybe we should settle for what we have. We agreed to be friends once before so let's try harder to keep to that.' She gave him a tremulous smile. 'I'd very much like to have you for a friend, David Ross.'

She turned away before he could say anything. Picking up the tray, she carried it from the room. David followed her out to the kitchen and waited while she put the tray on the table. She had that smile still fixed to her mouth when she turned to him, but it was so brittle that it made him ache just to see it.

He swung round without another word, let himself out of the house and made his way home. He was tired to the point of exhaustion from everything that had happened that day, but for a long time after he got into bed he couldn't sleep.

Thoughts danced round his brain, fragments of the past and the present which kept him tossing and turning as the hours passed. Yet when he finally drifted off to sleep it was Laura's face that filled his dreams, her voice he heard, her body he felt next to his. Laura, not Kate...

'You look like hell, David, if you don't mind me saying so.'

Sam propped himself against the door and regarded

him thoughtfully. David picked up a pen. He didn't need anyone to tell him how he looked because he had a pretty fair idea himself.

'Did you want something?' he asked shortly.

'I just thought you'd like to know that Andy made it all right.'

'Andy?' David queried, before realising with a rush that Sam was referring to the young climber. 'Oh, right. Good. What have the doctors said?'

'They're hopeful no permanent damage has occurred. I know one of the staff at Stoke—we trained together. And he told me that they're going to operate later today to fasten the bone ends together with metal wires.' Sam sighed. 'It's going to take months before Andy recovers and there might be some residual stiffness in the lower part of his back, but at least he'll have full use of his limbs, thanks to you.'

'It was a damned good job we all went last night.' David had shrugged off the compliment, though he was pleased to hear that the young man wouldn't be paralysed. 'It isn't often you end up with so many casualties all at once. I take it the others were OK?'

'Not too bad, considering. The girl with the fractured pelvis was the worst. I was really worried about her at one point. That's why I went in the ambulance with her. Fortunately, James followed on behind in my car so he drove us back.'

Sam hesitated and David had the impression that he was going to say something about Laura turning up, but in the end the locum didn't make any reference to her. David sighed heavily when Sam had departed. He trusted his friends not to go spreading gossip, but how long would it be before more rumours began circulating about him and Laura? And what sort of effect would they have on the children? Emily would have her hopes raised and he had no idea how Mike felt.

He buzzed Eileen to let her know that he was ready for his next patient. At some point soon he'd have to resolve the situation, but he had no idea how he was going to do that. He should by rights make it clear to Laura—and himself—that there was no future for them. And yet the thought of her going out of his life was more than he could bear...

CHAPTER TEN

DAVID was tied up in surgery all morning. The good weather had its drawbacks as several people turned up suffering from hay fever that day. Angela Harmon-King was one of them, and happened to be his last patient.

She came into the surgery, sneezing violently and dabbing her streaming eyes with a tissue. She and her husband owned a cottage in the town which they used for weekends, travelling up from London whenever they could. David was surprised to see her that day but it turned out that she and her husband had decided to take a week's holiday in Yewdale, something she was beginning to regret.

'I just can't stop sneezing, Dr Ross! And my eyes are driving me mad because they're so itchy...' She sneezed again as she sat down. She was in her early thirties, elegantly dressed in designer jeans and an expensive cashmere sweater, her blonde hair perfectly groomed. Only her swollen eyes and red-tipped nose spoiled the effect.

'The pollen count is high at the moment,' David sympathised. 'Is this the first time you've been so badly affected?'

'It is. I tend to get the odd bout back home but it's been worse than it's ever been in the past few days.' Angela sighed. 'I suppose it's being here that's done it, surrounded by all this greenery.'

'I expect so. What does your own doctor usually prescribe for you, Mrs Harmon-King?'

'I've brought the empty packet with me.' Angela passed it across the desk. 'I wouldn't have bothered you only when I popped into the chemist's yesterday to see if I could buy some more tablets I was told that they're available only on prescription. I was quite surprised as I've often bought hay-fever remedies over the counter in the past.'

'You still can buy a lot of hay-fever remedies without a prescription. However, these particular tablets contain a drug called terfenadine,' David explained, when he saw what Angela had been taking. 'Unfortunately, there have been a few problems in the past with people taking tablets containing terfenadine.'

'What sort of problems?' Angela looked startled. 'I mean, I've always found these really effective. I tried dozens of others before the doctor prescribed these for me a couple of years ago, but I usually found that they made me drowsy. These don't have that effect at all. In fact, I've never had any trouble since I started taking them.'

'I'm sure you haven't. Taken on its own, terfenadine is one of the most effective antihistamines available. However, it can react badly when taken in conjunction with certain antibacterial or antibiotic drugs.' David frowned, wondering what it was about that statement that rang a bell. There was a vague idea hovering at the back of his mind, but for the life of him he couldn't work out what it was.

'What do you mean, they can react badly?'

David forced himself to concentrate as he saw Angela's surprise. 'There have been a number of incidences of cardiac dysrhythmias and liver problems, which is why chemists are loath to sell tablets containing terfenadine without a prescription.'

'Good heavens! I had no idea.' Angela looked quite perturbed and David hastened to reassure her.

'I'm sure that they won't have caused you any problems at all so you mustn't worry. As I said, it's the interaction of terfenadine with certain other drugs that causes the trouble. So long as you take the tablets as instructed, they don't present a danger. However, I can prescribe something else if you'd prefer. There are several non-sedating products on the market now which should be suitable.'

'Oh, please! Although I don't know if I should take anything after what you've just told me.'

David shook his head. 'There's no point in putting up with all the discomfort when there are perfectly safe remedies available. Hay fever can be very distressing to those who suffer from it.' He wrote out a prescription and handed it to the woman. 'This one should be just as effective as your usual tablets and it doesn't carry the same risk of side-effects.'

After Angela Harmon-King had left, David set about clearing up. However, he couldn't shake off the feeling that he was missing something. He stopped stock still as the reason hit him, before hurrying out to the desk where Eileen was busily dealing with the morning's paperwork.

'Have you got Cyril Rogerson's notes there, please, Eileen? I just want to take a look at them.'

He carried the notes back to his room and sat down at his desk to read through them, pausing as he came to one entry. It was a note that Cyril had visited a doctor in Norwich a few months previously, complain-

ing of a sore throat, and had been prescribed a course
of erythromycin!

David sat back in the chair, his head buzzing with
possibilities. Cyril suffered from hay fever so was it
possible that his trouble stemmed from combining a
hay-fever remedy containing terfenadine with the
erythromycin, which was one of the antibiotics known
to trigger an adverse reaction? The only flaw in the
idea was that Cyril had never been prescribed any such
hay-fever medication at the surgery so where would he
have got hold of the tablets?

It was a long shot but David had a feeling that it
might be the missing link he'd been searching for. He
went back to the office and checked the *British
National Formulary*, the guide to all drugs they prescribed in the course of their work. It gave a clear
warning against prescribing the two drugs in conjunction, plus a list of possible side-effects—a lot of which
mirrored the symptoms he'd seen in Cyril Rogerson!

'I'm going over to the pottery, Eileen. I shouldn't be
long, but if anyone wants me that's where I'll be.'

'Right you are.' Eileen looked puzzled but David
didn't waste time, explaining. He wanted to speak to
Cyril as soon as he could to see if he could clear up
the mystery of the man's illness.

Cyril was on his dinner break when David got there.
He was obviously surprised to see him and faintly
alarmed when David asked if he could have a word
with him.

'What is it, Dr Ross? Have them there blood tests
come back? Is it something really bad?'

'They're not back yet, Cyril. However, I've had an
idea about what could be wrong with you. I just need
you to tell me which hay-fever tablets you take.' David

mentally crossed his fingers, and was disappointed when Cyril told him the brand name as it wasn't one containing terfenadine, as he'd hoped.

'I see. Well, it looks as though I was wrong after all.' He sighed. 'I had an idea that it might be the hay-fever tablets you were taking combined with the anti-biotic the doctor in Norwich prescribed for you, although I imagine he would have checked if you were on any other medication.'

Cyril frowned. 'I do recall him asking if I was taking anything…but now I come to think of it, my hay fever didn't start up until after I saw the doctor there. It began a day or so later. I didn't have any of my tablets with me but our Sarah had some so I took them to save trailing all the way back into town. But she's taken the same ones for years now,' he added, 'and she's never had any problems so I can't see as it's them.'

'Can you remember what they were—the tablets Sarah gave you to take?' David asked quickly.

'I'm not sure…' Cyril frowned and smiled as he suddenly remembered. David felt like cheering when Cyril told him the name of a tablet containing terfenadine.

'I think we just might have found the answer to why you've been feeling so ill lately, Cyril. I suspect that the interaction of the terfenadine in the hay-fever remedy and the erythromycin you were prescribed for your throat has caused all the trouble. I'm going to get straight on to the hospital and have a word with the consultant there to see what he recommends. I'm only sorry that I didn't see the link sooner.'

'You weren't to know, Dr Ross.' Cyril looked slightly bemused by events. 'Nor was that doctor I saw while I was at our Sarah's. He did ask me if I was taking anything else. If it's anyone's fault then it's mine, but I never gave it a thought when I took those tablets. Who'd believe they could cause so much harm, eh?'

'Well, it isn't certain yet but I do think we could be on the right track at last. I'll be in touch as soon as I hear what the hospital has to say.'

David drove back to the surgery and put a call straight through to the consultant at the hospital, who immediately suggested that Cyril should be admitted the following day. He telephoned the pottery and told Cyril the news, explaining that he'd need to undergo a series of tests. If Cyril's liver had been poisoned by the combination of the two drugs then it was imperative that he receive treatment right away.

David put down the phone after he had finished the call. It was good to think that he'd got to the bottom of the problem at last. If only all problems could be worked out so satisfactorily, but maybe it was expecting too much to find an easy solution to his personal problems. The situation between him and Laura was just too complicated and bound up with so many other things that getting to the real heart of it seemed impossibly difficult. And yet why should it be so hard? He should be honest and look at how he felt about her...

He sighed as he got up from the desk. Maybe he already knew how he felt but that didn't make it feel right. The only thing he could still give Kate was his loyalty. Surely that wasn't asking too much?

The days drifted past. Laura didn't make any attempt to contact him, though he knew she was still at her house. Obviously, she wanted him to understand that the decision was in his hands. When Emily asked if she could go over and help Laura do some painting on Thursday, he didn't have the heart to refuse. Why should he spoil his daughter's happiness just because he was so mixed up?

Friday arrived and David went into work feeling more restless than ever. Everyone was gathered in the staffroom, drinking coffee and discussing what they had planned for the coming weekend. Elizabeth had invited James's parents to visit them and was busily working out where they would take the older couple so that they could see as much of the countryside around Yewdale as possible.

David was pleased that everything was going so well for his friends, but he couldn't dispel the black cloud that seemed to be hovering over him. Maybe he needed a complete change, he thought, going over to the window to stare out at the familiar view. Maybe he should think about leaving the town that held so many memories and starting afresh somewhere else.

With Laura? the voice of temptation whispered. Would it be easier to start a new life away from Yewdale? Or would this guilt haunt him wherever he went?

'What's the matter, David?'

He glanced round as Elizabeth came to join him, forcing a smile as he saw her concern. 'Nothing. Why? Do I look as though something is wrong?'

'Yes, frankly, you do.' Elizabeth glanced over her shoulder and lowered her voice so the others couldn't hear. 'I've sensed that something has been troubling you for some time now. If there's anything I can do then just tell me.'

'Thanks. I'll remember that.' He took a quick swallow of coffee and smiled tautly 'However, I'm fine, honestly. Probably could do with a change, that's all. Maybe I should think about taking a holiday. It would be good for the kids to get away for a week or so.'

'You could be right. But I'm here if you feel like talking.' Elizabeth glanced across the room at James and her face softened. 'I know how confusing it can be, believe me.'

David frowned as she moved away. What had she meant by that? How confusing *what* could be? Abbie came over just then to have a word with him about Mrs Walsh, who was being sent home from hospital later that week, but his mind was only partly on the problem of how much care they could provide for the old lady.

His thoughts kept returning to what Elizabeth had said. Had she been referring to what was going on between him and Laura? But how could she know anything about the situation? Oh, Elizabeth must have heard the gossip—as they all had—but she was too sensible to take much heed of it. So what had she meant!

'The hospital rang while you were out, David. I took the call for you.' James popped his head round the consulting room door. 'Evidently, they've discovered that Cyril Rogerson's liver is badly swollen. Working along the guidelines you gave them, they're convinced that it's been the two drugs which have caused it. They've put him on an intravenous drip and are keeping him under observation.'

'So I was right!' David tossed his pen onto the desk with a sigh of relief. It was Friday afternoon and evening surgery was due to start in half an hour. It had been a hectic day and he'd only just arrived back from doing some house calls. However, to hear that Cyril's problem was being dealt with brought relief. 'I never thought I'd get to the bottom of that case at one point!'

'I know. Sometimes you have the devil of a job working it out, don't you? Still, you turned up trumps this time, from the sound of it.' James started to back out of the room then paused. 'Oh, before I forget. Beth wants to know if she can borrow Emily tomorrow afternoon. She wants to take her to the dressmaker's to have her measured for her bridesmaid's dress.'

'Of course. No problem.' David waited until James had gone before he picked up the phone, guiltily aware that he hadn't remembered to tell Emily about her being a bridesmaid at the coming wedding. Emily herself answered the phone and he smiled as he heard her clear little voice.

'Dr Ross's house. Emily speaking. Can I help you?'

'Well, hello, there, sweetheart. Guess who this is?'

'Daddy! I was going to ring you but now I don't need to, do I? Can I go to tea at Laura's? She said I could but only if I asked you first. Here, you speak to her then you can tell her that it's all right!'

The phone must have changed hands at that point because before David could say anything Laura came on the line. His breath caught as he recognised her voice. Suddenly, it was as though she was in the room with him and he could actually see her—those delicately perfect features, that soft blonde hair, her warmth and vitality which drew him like a magnet.

'I didn't mean to put you on the spot like this, David.'

The flatness of her voice brought him back to the present with a rush. David felt his heart ache as he heard those sweetly husky tones now devoid of feeling.

Laura was trying her hardest to stick to the guidelines of being a friend, as they'd agreed, but at what cost?

'You're not.' His own town was equally flat because he was afraid of giving away how he felt if he didn't control his emotions. 'It's very good of you to invite her. Are you sure it isn't any trouble, though?'

'Of course not. I'll put her back on so she can speak to you.' Laura was gone before he could say anything else but, then, what could he have said? Maybe it was easier and simpler if they tried to behave as neighbours did.

He felt a sudden wash of heat run through his veins as he recalled what had happened between them. How could they go back to being distant after that?

'Daddy... Are you still there?'

He shook his head to clear the disturbing thoughts from it as he heard Emily's anxious voice. 'Yes, I'm still here, poppet. I've told Laura that it's OK if you go to her house, but you're to be good, mind. No getting in her way or pestering her.'

'Course not!' Emily assured him blithely. 'I'll see you later, then. Bye!'

The receiver was replaced with a crash that made him wince. He hung up at his end, realising belatedly that he still hadn't told Emily about the treat which was in store for her. He sighed as he picked up a pen. When he spoke to Laura it did tend to put everything else out of his head!

It was almost eight when he got home that night. Several patients had turned up at the last minute, making them run over time. David slammed the car door and hesitated, but there was no way he could avoid going next door. Emily had been with Laura long enough and he didn't want the child outstaying her welcome.

Peebody gave his customary bark when he knocked, but David knew by now that it was all show. There wasn't a vicious bone in the animal's body, a feeling which was reinforced as the door opened and Peebody came to greet him wearing a bonnet taken from one of Emily's rarely played-with dolls.

He bent to fondle the dog's nose, using the few seconds to adjust to the fact that Laura was standing right in front of him. It seemed like half a lifetime since he'd seen her last so his mind swirled as all his senses were assailed by the sight and sound and smell of her.

'Come in. Emily's just finishing icing a cake she's made. I think it's meant to be a surprise for you so be warned.'

Laura stepped aside to admit him to the hall. She reached past him to close the door just as Peebody jumped up to lavish a welcoming lick on David. He staggered sideways, bumping right into Laura and almost knocking her over.

'Sorry!' He reached out to steady her, his hands lightly gripping her arms. She was wearing a sleeveless cotton T-shirt in a vivid citrus green with a simple white skirt. The warmth of her skin seemed to flow right through his fingertips and spread through his body, making his blood stir.

How could simply holding Laura like this cause such mayhem? he wondered dazedly, then stopped thinking at all as she suddenly moved so that unwittingly his hand brushed her breast.

David's eyes dropped to where his fingers lay so softly against her and he saw her nipple peak under the thin cotton fabric. Her immediate response brought about an answering one in himself as he felt his body quicken painfully.

His eyes flew to her face and he saw the expression that darkened her eyes, a mixture of hunger and need mingled with the shimmering, heart-stopping warmth of her love. Suddenly there was no doubt in his mind as to how she felt about him. Laura loved him. It was the sweetest kind of torment possible to know that.

'Come on through to the kitchen.' She broke away from him, her movements jerky as she quickly led the way along the hall. David followed more slowly, striving to get himself in check, but it was hard to control this hunger he felt, this simple but overwhelming longing to *do* something about what he'd seen in Laura's eyes just now!

'See what I've made, Daddy!' Emily carefully picked up the cake from the table and held it out for his inspection. David somehow managed to smile.

'Why, that's lovely. I can't wait to have a piece of it.'

'I can't cut it yet 'cos the icing's still all runny.' Emily carefully put the plate back on the table and tested the shocking pink icing with her finger, leaving a dimple in it. She licked the sugary smear off her finger, before explaining importantly, 'Laura said it would be better if I left it till tomorrow so it can set.'

'Well, I'm sure she's right.' It took every scrap of composure David possessed—plus some he didn't know he was capable of—to act normally as he turned to Laura. 'Thanks for having Emily round tonight. I hope she hasn't been any trouble.'

'Of course not,' Laura replied politely. She smiled more easily as the little girl went and hugged her. Laura hugged the child back, glancing at David over the top of Emily's head. 'I've loved having her here, to be honest.'

'I wish I could stay here all night with you, Laura.' Emily turned huge, dark eyes on David. 'Wouldn't you like to stay as well, Daddy?'

Out of the mouths of babes, indeed! David could feel himself going hot as he struggled to find an appropriate answer, but it was Laura who defused the situation when she laughed. Her blue eyes were full of wry amusement as she glanced at him, before turning her attention back to the child.

'I'm sure your daddy is very tired after working so hard all day but if you'd like to stay then you can, Emily. Then Daddy can have a nice quiet evening all to himself.'

'Can I? Really?' Emily's face lit up. She turned imploringly to David. 'Can I stay with Laura tonight? Please, please, Daddy!'

'Well, I'm not sure...' David frowned, not sure it was a good idea. Emily was getting more and more attached to Laura, which was the last thing he wanted. He sighed. 'I am on call tonight so I suppose so.'

He'd barely got the words out before Emily rushed over to give him a hug, too. When Laura told her which bedroom she could use she went racing out of the room and they could hear her running up the stairs with Peebody at her heels.

'I suppose I shouldn't have offered to let her stay. I'm sorry—' Laura began but David cut her off.

'No, it's OK. I just don't want her becoming a nuisance.'

'She isn't. She's a lovely child, David, and I enjoy her company.' Laura glanced around, seemingly uneasy now that they were alone. 'What time do you want her back home tomorrow?'

'Oh, eight will be fine. I'm due in surgery in the morning but Emily can come with me. Mike was saying something about wanting to play cricket. She'll be happy enough in the staffroom, drawing. By the way, where's Mike, do you know? I noticed there weren't any lights on when I drove up. Did he happen to mention where he was going?'

'He said he was going round to his friend's house once he knew Emily was coming over here. I don't know who he meant, though.'

'Probably Danny Shepherd. I expect he's left me a note.' David sighed. 'I often wonder if I put too much responsibility on him by expecting him to mind Emily when I'm at work. But there isn't a choice, apart from getting someone in to stay with her until I get home. Maybe I'll have to think about doing that soon—' He broke off, realising that none of this was Laura's concern.

'Well, I won't keep you. Thanks again for having Emily.' He turned to leave, pausing when Laura suddenly spoke.

'Have you eaten yet? I could make you something, if you'd like.'

David gripped the doorknob as he struggled with temptation. 'Thanks, but I don't think that would be a good idea.'

'Because it might start off the gossip again?' Laura gave a strained little laugh which cut him to the quick. He swung round so fast that he saw her take an involuntary step back. He had no idea what was on his face at that moment but he saw her eyes darken.

'I don't give a damn about the gossip, Laura!' His

voice cut like a lash and he saw her flinch. 'But I do care about what might happen. If I stayed for something to eat then I just might not find enough strength to go home afterwards.'

He wrenched the door open, leaving her standing there. What wouldn't he have given to turn round and go back to accept everything she would offer him so willingly…so lovingly. Only he knew in his heart how wrong that would be. He couldn't take from Laura until he could give her something in return.

Mike was home again when David opened the door. He had brought his friend, Danny, back with him and both of them were sprawled in the sitting-room, listening to music. David put his head round the door to let Mike know he was in, and the music was lowered by several decibels. When Mike discovered that Emily was staying overnight at Laura's he asked if he could go back to Danny's and stay the night there.

David agreed at once, breathing a sigh of relief as the music was abruptly switched off and the two boys disappeared. Peace at last! However, it didn't last long. He'd no sooner made himself something to eat than the phone rang. It was Lucy Fleming to say that Ben wasn't well.

David drove straight over to the Flemings' house and soon discovered that Ben had croup. He had all the classic signs, coughing and grunting when he tried to breathe.

'He was right as rain before, Dr Ross.' John Fleming gently nursed his baby son, his face full of concern. 'We put him down for the night and then he started crying and couldn't seem to breathe properly.'

'Croup usually flares up like that and, more often than not, at night, too. It's caused by the narrowing and inflammation of the airways, usually due to some sort of mild viral infection. It's extremely common in infants so don't be too alarmed,' David explained.

He turned to Lucy, who was looking very worried as she listened to the baby's rasping breathing. 'Can you go and run the bath, Lucy? And keep the bathroom door closed so that the room gets really steamy. The best cure for croup is to take Ben into a steamy room as the moist air will help him breathe more easily. And do try to stay calm. Ben can sense you're upset and it will only make things worse.'

It took some time but the steam treatment gradually worked and Ben was breathing easily by the time David left the Flemings' house.

Another call came through almost as soon as he reached home so he set off once more for the Outward Bound centre this time, which was set on the banks of Yewdale Water, a couple of miles outside the town. One of the children who was staying there had been violently sick and was complaining of stomach pains.

David wasn't at all happy with what he found, suspecting that the thirteen-year-old girl had possible appendicitis. Ian Farnsworth, the centre manager, immediately offered to drive the child to hospital rather than wait for an ambulance.

David felt far happier once he'd waved them off, with Ian's wife, Barbara, sitting in the back with the child. There wasn't any point in taking chances where appendicitis was concerned and it was better to err on the side of caution rather than run the risk of the appendix perforating.

It was well after midnight when he got home again. He went straight up to bed, worn out by the hectic day.

He was just stripping off his shirt when there was a knock at the front door.

What now? David thought as he hurriedly put his shirt back on and ran down to answer it. Laura was standing on the step, her face very pale in the wash of light flowing out from the hall.

'It's Emily,' she said without any preamble. 'Can you come and take a look at her, David?'

David felt his heart spasm with fear. 'What's the matter with her? Has there been an accident?'

'No.' Laura took a deep breath. 'I think it could be meningitis. We need to get her to hospital straight away.'

CHAPTER ELEVEN

'WE'LL be doing the lumbar puncture in a few minutes. Do you want to see Emily now?'

'Yes.' David felt as though he'd aged twenty years in the past couple of hours. His legs would hardly support him as he got up to follow Laura into the small side-room. Emily looked so small and ill as she lay in the big hospital bed that he felt his eyes fill.

'She was put on an intravenous drip of antibiotics as soon as she was admitted so they should be taking effect even now.' Laura's tone was clinically detached as she outlined the little girl's treatment. 'We're assuming that it's a strain of bacterial meningitis as the symptoms developed so rapidly.'

'She was fine when I saw her tonight...' David blinked hard as he recalled Emily showing off the cake she'd made. He touched her hand but she was deeply unconscious and had no idea that he was there.

'She was.' Laura's voice had a catch in it despite how hard she was trying to maintain her professional composure. 'It's incredible how quickly it all developed. She came downstairs around ten o'clock and said she felt hot and that her head hurt. Then shortly after that she was very sick. I tried phoning you but you were out on a call.

'I sat with her for the next hour or so and she complained that her neck was stiff when I helped her sit up to give her a drink. Also, there were definite signs of photophobia when I switched on the overhead light to examine her. I phoned the hospital immediately and put them on stand-by. I was just about to drive her here when I saw your bedroom light go on and realised you were back.'

'Thank God you recognised the symptoms so quickly.' David took Laura's hand and held it. 'She will pull through, won't she? Because she's received such prompt treatment, that must have increased her chances of recovery?'

'We're going to do everything we can for Emily, David, believe me.' Laura's own eyes were misty as she squeezed his hand. They both looked round as the door opened. Another doctor and a nurse came into the room with a trolley bearing what was needed to perform the lumbar puncture.

Laura turned to him again, her blue eyes full of compassion. 'Perhaps it might be better if you leave Dr Blake and I to get on with this, David. I know how hard it is for you.'

'No.' He managed a smile to soften his refusal because he knew that Laura only wanted to spare his feelings. 'I want to stay with Emily and be here for her.'

Laura didn't say anything more. She and the other doctor quietly set about the task of drawing off a little spinal fluid via a hollow needle inserted into the spinal canal. It was a delicate job and David breathed more easily once it was completed. Emily was still unconscious but he sat by the side of her bed holding her hand as the room cleared.

Laura murmured something about taking the sample straight to the lab but David was only half listening by that point. He was willing Emily to get better, willing the drugs to fight the infection. He couldn't lose her. He couldn't bear it.

The night passed and he must have fallen asleep just before dawn. He was woken when a nurse came in a short time later to take Emily's pulse and check the drip. He got up and went to the window, trying to ease the cramp from his stiff muscles as the nurse quietly set about changing the almost empty bag of antibiotics for a fresh one.

The city spread before him, grey and sombre in the early morning light, and he was beset by a sudden yearning to be back home in Yewdale surrounded by the greenness of the mountains.

If only he could turn back the clock so that this had never happened, he thought wistfully. But it was impossible to go backwards in time. He had to look forwards, to when Emily was better and he was able to take her home again.

Time was relentless as it moved on and it was a sin to waste his life without living every day to the full. Kate had lived her life that way, right up until the last precious moment. The thought brought him some measure of comfort, although he wasn't sure why it should.

'David.'

He hadn't realised that Laura had come into the room until she spoke. He turned and saw the lines of tiredness etched into her face. She'd stayed all night, too, although she'd made no attempt to join him at Emily's bedside. Had she thought that she wouldn't be welcome? he wondered. That he preferred to be on his own with his daughter? Didn't Laura know that she was already so much a part of his life that he couldn't imagine a future without her?

The realisation settled softly into his mind, causing

barely a stir. He wasn't even aware of opening his arms to her until he closed them around her. He buried his face in the sweetness of her hair and felt as though he'd come home after a long and tiring journey. Laura was home and comfort and love and so much more that he couldn't put a name to half of it. But there was one thing he could do and one thing he could tell her which she would understand.

Her eyes were very blue as he raised her chin, the uncertainty in them making his heart ache at what she must have been going through these past weeks. He cupped her cheek, his own eyes full of everything he felt, and he heard the small indrawn breath she took even before he'd said what he wanted to.

'I love you, Laura.'

So few words and yet what power they had. He watched as joy transformed her face and chased away the shadows, felt it touch his own heart which had been dead for so long. He loved Laura. He felt no shame nor guilt in admitting it any longer. Kate would have been the first to tell him that!

He bent to kiss her, a kiss of love and tenderness and simple relief that she was there for him when he needed her most of all. He let her go almost immediately because it simply wasn't the time or the place for anything more than this token. But it was enough to be going on with—far more than he'd ever believed he would be capable of giving her!

They both stayed with Emily, talking a little but not really needing to. Confirmation came through that Emily had meningococcal meningitis—one of the rare strains—which meant that Emily's school would need to be alerted and vaccinations offered to anyone she'd come into contact with.

David telephoned Mike and told him what had happened, trying his best to reassure his son. He then had to phone Elizabeth and explain that he wouldn't be able to cover surgery that morning. He wasn't really surprised when both James and Sam appeared at the hospital later that morning, bringing Mike with them. Elizabeth was covering for him and sent her love and her assurances that they could manage without him for however long he needed to stay at the hospital.

David realised how lucky he was to have so many people who cared about him and his family. But the best thing of all was that he had Laura there, quietly giving him her support and love. When Emily started to show definite signs of improvement around teatime he felt truly blessed.

He went to the bed and took hold of her hand, smiling down into her wan little face. 'Hello, monster. You gave us all a real scare.'

'Did I?' Emily tried to smile through dry, cracked lips. 'I'm thirsty, Daddy. Can I have a drink, please?'

'Here, let me get it.' Laura poured some water into a beaker and let the child drink a little of it through the spout.

Emily frowned in disgust. 'Only babies have cups like that, and I'm not a baby!'

'No, but you have been very, very poorly. Mike's waiting outside. Do you want to see him for a moment?' David suggested to distract her.

'Yes, please.' Emily looked round. 'Is Peebody here as well? Can I see him, too?'

'I'm afraid he wasn't allowed to come to the hospital,' Laura explained, 'but he's sent you a big lick and says that you're to get better soon. Abbie is looking after him while I'm here so I hope he's being good for her.'

'Did you tell her to leave a night-light on for him?' Emily sounded worried. 'You know how scared he is of the dark.'

'I did. So don't you worry about him.' Laura glanced at David. 'I'll send Mike in, shall I?'

It was obvious that she thought they might like some time on their own, but David had no intention of allowing her to think that. He took hold of her hand. 'We'll both tell him.'

Mike looked relieved when David explained that his sister was awake and on the road to recovery. He hurried in to see her while David led Laura along the corridor to a small waiting area, which was empty for once. Once out of sight of anyone passing, he drew her into his arms and kissed her as he'd been aching to do for hours.

He drew back and rested his forehead against hers, drinking in the warmth and fragrance of her skin. 'I could tell you this a hundred times and still not tire of saying it—I love you, Laura Mackenzie.'

'Do you?' she queried softly, yet there was an odd note in her voice which disturbed him. David frowned as he drew back to look at her. At that moment they heard footsteps in the corridor and then a nurse suddenly popped her head round the door.

'Sorry to interrupt you, Dr Mackenzie, but Ryan Cassidy's parents are making a bit of a fuss about why his treatment has been delayed until next week. Could you come and have a word with them, do you think?'

'Of course, Ruth. I'll be right there.' Laura waited until the nurse had gone, before turning to David. 'I think we need to talk about what's happened, David,' she said with her customary forthrightness. 'Obviously, we can't do that here when there are so many distractions. I think it would be better if we put all this on hold until Emily is fully recovered.'

'Of course.' David could hear the stiffly formal note in his voice but he couldn't help it. What did Laura want to talk about? Had he been wrong about her feelings after all? Had she realised that *she'd* been wrong about them, perhaps?

He felt his stomach sink at the thought but there was no way he could broach the question at that moment. Laura didn't say anything more as she hurried from the room, but David didn't follow her. He stood in the centre of the room and his heart felt like a lead weight as he considered yet another possibility.

Maybe he'd taken too long deciding how he felt so that Laura's feelings had changed. Maybe he'd come to his senses too late.

The next week seemed to be a never-ending succession of days which were all the same. David spent all his time with Emily, talking or reading to her and playing endless games to fill in the hours. Elizabeth and James had urged him to take as much time off work as he needed, but sometimes, as when Emily was napping, he would have given anything to have his work to concentrate on rather than the thoughts that plagued him constantly.

Laura was a regular visitor, although Emily was no longer under her care. Several times each day she came to visit the child and spent a few minutes talking to her. David both looked forward to and dreaded these visits because he was usually left in such turmoil afterwards.

Did Laura love him—really love him? Or had he simply misconstrued her feelings? He had no idea and she never gave him any clue as to how she felt. She was polite yet impersonal when they spoke, and he felt her withdrawal all the more sharply because it was such a contrast to how she'd behaved in the past.

Once it was certain that Emily wasn't going to suffer any repercussions from her illness David decided to go back to work. Emily would be discharged the following week in all likelihood, and she was well enough now not to need him at her bedside constantly. Her school friends had sent her a huge get-well card they'd made for her, and her teacher had been in to visit her as well.

David had a feeling that she was enjoying all the fuss being made of her so he was confident that she wouldn't miss having him around.

It felt strange at first, going back into work after such a lengthy absence, but after a couple of hours he soon settled back into the routine. Every patient he saw asked after Emily and offered their best wishes for her recovery. Marie Rogerson popped in just to leave a little present for Emily, a fluffy blue duck with a bright orange beak. Evidently Cyril was still in hospital but the doctors there were confident that he'd make a full recovery in time.

David was delighted that things had worked out all right in such a puzzling case and appreciative that Marie had found the time to think about Emily. It was good to know that so many people cared. It made him realize that, whatever else happened, he wanted to stay in Yewdale and remain part of the community. But would he be able to face living next door to Laura? That was a question he couldn't answer until he spoke to her.

He felt as though he was marking time until the weekend arrived, yet when he heard her car coming down the lane late on Friday night he was beset by nerves. He went to the window, watching her headlights lighting up the night sky as she turned into her drive.

What if Laura didn't want anything more to do with him? What if she didn't love him and he'd been mistaken all along? What if—?

'You OK, Dad?'

He swung away from the window, summoning a strained smile when he saw Mike standing in the doorway. Mike had been round at Danny's again that evening and he hadn't heard him come in. 'Yes, of course. Did you have a good time? You seem to be spending a lot of time with Danny lately—what are you two up to?'

'Oh, this and that. You know.' Mike shrugged. He looked down at his feet then took a deep breath as though he had something he wanted to say and wasn't finding it easy. 'Look, Dad, I know parents always think they know everything but sometimes they can be really dense.'

David's brows rose. 'Is that a fact? And am I guilty of that?'

'Uh-huh.' Mike ran a hand through his dark brown hair. David suddenly realised that his son had grown a good few inches recently and was as tall as he was now. Mike was no longer a child, but growing up fast, and what he said next simply reinforced that.

'Look, Dad, I don't know why you're making such a big deal out of this. So you fancy Laura and she fancies you—what's the problem? Seems to me that the pair of you should try getting your act together.'

'I…' David was stumped for words. Was it so obvious how he felt about Laura? His heart gave a juddering lurch. Was it so obvious how she felt about him?

Mike gave him a cocky grin, still young enough to enjoy disconcerting his parent. 'Go with the flow, Dad. Laura's cool, you know what I mean?'

David nodded because he didn't trust himself to speak. In his own way, Mike was giving him his blessing and telling him that he didn't mind if David acted on his feelings for Laura. He went and gave the boy a quick hug, letting him go almost immediately as he sensed Mike's embarrassment at such a display of affection.

Mike took himself off to his room and music came thundering down through the floorboards a few minutes later, making the whole house shake. David took a deep breath and squared his shoulders. 'Go with the flow' was it? Well, he'd have to see how good he was at that!

There was a light on in the kitchen. David rapped on the door and waited, with his heart thumping, for Laura to answer. He heard Peebody bark and Laura's voice issuing from somewhere, telling the dog to be quiet.

The door opened and there she was. David felt as though he were going to explode as he saw her. She had on the same outfit she'd worn the very first time he'd seen her—denim dungarees and a check shirt— only this time the paint spattered all over her was a delicate shade of eau-de-Nil.

For a moment they both merely stood and looked at one another then Laura held the door wide open. 'Come in.'

He heard the tremor in her voice and for some reason

it brought his confidence surging back. Suddenly he knew what he was going to say and do, how he was going to handle this. He loved Laura Mackenzie and by heaven he was going to tell her so. And then she was going to tell him how she felt.

Something of what he was thinking must have shown because he saw faint colour rise to her face before she turned away abruptly. She picked up the kettle and went to the sink to fill it, talking over her shoulder to avoid looking at him. 'How about some tea? I was just going to have some—'

She stopped dead and her blue eyes were huge as he calmly lifted the kettle from her grasp. 'I don't want tea. And I don't want coffee either.' He smiled, watching her colour deepen. 'Would you like to hear what I *do* want, darling?'

'I... You... Are you sure, David?' There was no pretence that she didn't understand what he meant, but that was typical of her. Was there ever a woman so honest, so frank, so...so completely and utterly lovable?

He pulled her into his arms with a speed that made her gasp. 'Yes, I'm sure! I love you, Laura Mackenzie—every tiny bit of you! Now, put me out of my misery and tell me that you adore me, too.'

'I do.' Her eyes swam with sudden tears as they met his. 'I love you so much, David, that I don't think there are enough words in the world to tell you how I feel.'

'That's all I wanted to hear.' He bent and kissed her, the hunger he'd held in check for so long suddenly released into one burning kiss which left both of them trembling when it ended.

Laura nestled her head into his shoulder, her hands running over his back as though she were absorbing the feel of him. 'I never thought you'd admit it. I thought that I was wishing for the moon by hoping for this from you.'

'Because of Kate?' He felt overcome with tenderness as he lifted her face to meet his gaze. 'At one point I thought that too, Laura. I was tormented by the thought that I was betraying Kate, by falling in love with you, which is why I fought against it for so long.'

He stroked her cheek with a gentle finger, loving the feel of her silky skin, smiling at the paint splatters which adorned it. She was so beautiful that he could have stood there all night and simply looked at her, but there were other pleasures to enjoy as well as that.

His hand ran down her spine as he drew her closer and let her feel the effect of what holding her was doing to him, and he heard the swift indrawn breath she took. There was a husky note to her soft voice when she spoke again. 'But now you're sure that this is what you want, David, and that you won't feel guilty about it in the future?'

'Yes, I'm sure. I knew at the hospital that morning after Emily was taken ill. I realised then that not living each and every day to its fullest was a worse betrayal of Kate and all she believed in.' His eyes were adoring as they held hers. 'I knew that Kate would have wanted me to be happy with you and that there wasn't any reason for me to deny how I felt any longer.'

'Did you? I was so afraid...' Laura bit her lip, as though suddenly shy of explaining, but David urged her on.

'Of what? What were you afraid of, Laura? I sensed something had happened but I couldn't understand what it was.' His voice caught as he recalled his be-wilderment and how it had hurt to imagine she didn't love him. 'I was terrified that I'd wasted so much time that you no longer cared for me.'

'No! Oh, David, how could you think that?' Laura reached up and kissed him, wanting him to believe that she meant every word. 'I was just scared that you'd regret what you said once everything had calmed down again. With Emily being so ill, it put you under a tremendous strain and I know how that can affect people and make them behave as they might not normally do. I…I was afraid to believe what you said in case you changed your mind later. I couldn't have stood that!'

'Oh, my darling, no! It wasn't just what happened to Emily, although it did help me see the situation clearly for the first time.' He brushed her mouth with a kiss, tempted to linger a moment or two longer but this needed clearing up first.

'I think I knew that I was in love with you ages before that, but I couldn't admit it either to you or to myself. It was all bound up with the guilt I felt over Kate's death. But all that's in the past now. Kate will always be a very special part of my life because I loved her. I never thought I could ever love another woman again until I met you.'

He laughed softly as he twined a golden curl round his finger and tugged it gently. 'You came into my life in your dungarees and all spattered with paint and caused an instant upheaval. I didn't know if I was on my head or my heels, to be honest, as you had a knack of saying things which completely threw me. I have a feeling that isn't going to change, but I expect I can put up with it.'

He laughed as she gasped in outrage, kissing her quickly to avert the storm which was brewing. 'When we made love that morning I knew then that I was under your spell, but I was still fighting against it. I don't intend to fight any more. I love you, Laura, with my heart and my soul—with every bit of me. Is that enough to convince you that I won't change my mind?'

'Nearly!' She whipped out of his arms so fast that David had no chance of stopping her. She made her way to the door and held out her hand. 'I think I know of a way which might just tip the scales all the way.'

David laughed as he went to join her. He paused to glance down at Peebody and shook his head as the dog tried to follow them. 'No way, Peebody. You stay here. This is something Laura and I can sort out for ourselves!'

'And my dress is blue with frills round the neck and a huge petti-…petti-something!'

'Petticoat.' David laughed at Emily's excitement. She was just back from her first fitting at the dressmaker's for her bridesmaid's dress and was very excited about it. It was wonderful to see her so lively again after how ill she'd been. David found it hard to believe that this was the same child who just a few weeks ago had lain unconscious in a hospital bed.

'Chloe's dress is going to be the same as mine, but Abbie's is different. Elizabeth showed us her dress as well but I can't tell you what it's like 'cos it's a secret,' Emily explained importantly, then glanced round as she heard Peebody barking a greeting as he and Laura slipped through the hedge. She ran over to Laura and told her all about her dress once again then went off to find a ball to play with the dog.

'She's really thrilled about this wedding, isn't she?' Laura said as she came and sat down beside David on the bench.

He slipped his arm around her shoulders and pulled her to him, kissing her quickly on the cheek. 'She is. It's so wonderful to see that she's made a full recovery like that, thanks to you, Laura.' He tilted her face, loving the way her eyes immediately darkened with emotion as she looked at him. There was a catch in his voice when he spoke. 'Kate gave me Emily and you gave her back to me. I can't tell you how much that means to me.'

'Darling…' Laura kissed him tenderly. The kiss promised to go on for quite some time only at that moment Emily appeared with Peebody following close behind. The two were inseparable now and the dog remained at David's house when Laura went back to town.

'Daddy, I've been thinking,' Emily said, looking quizzically from him to Laura.

'Hmm, that sounds ominous,' David joked. 'What about?'

'Only that maybe I could use my bridesmaid's dress when you and Laura get married. Can I?'

David laughed softly. He glanced at Laura and raised his brows. 'What do you think about that idea?'

'That it's a very good one indeed. However, it would mean we'd have to wait until after Elizabeth marries James, and I don't know how you feel about that, David.'

'I'm open to suggestions, shall we say?' David felt his heart turn over as he looked into Laura's laughing face. They hadn't discussed getting married yet. Somehow it hadn't seemed important. It had been enough these past weeks just knowing Laura loved him and loving her in return. Suddenly he knew that he wanted it all, wanted their commitment to be official.

'Well, I just happened to call into the registrar's office on my way here yesterday. There was a really helpful lady there who told me that we could be married by special licence if we wanted to.' Laura kissed him quickly. 'It's up to you, of course, but I do happen to have a window in my schedule for next Saturday. Do you think you could make it for then?'

'I'm sure I can!' David pulled her into his arms, barely aware that Emily had gone rushing off in search of Mike to tell him the news. The kiss was long and infinitely satisfying, and when it was over David's mind was spinning so that he had to reassure himself that he hadn't dreamt the whole thing.

He set Laura a little away from him so he could think straight. 'You are sure that you don't want a white wedding like Elizabeth is having?'

'David, the only thing I *want* is you! Let's not wait any longer.' Her tone was husky with love and David closed his eyes as it hit him how lucky he was to have found her. He stood up, sliding his arm around her shoulders as they made their way to the house to tell Mike and Emily that the wedding would go ahead the following Saturday. He wasn't in any doubt that both children would be delighted, although how Holly was going to view the news he wasn't sure.

'Maybe we can find some way to get a message to Holly.' Once again Laura had seemed to read his mind, and he loved her even more for it.

He stopped and drew her into his arms, holding her to his heart where she would always be. 'I was just thinking that. There must be a way to get in touch with her. I'll see if the British Embassy can help.' He kissed her quickly. 'Just think, in seven days' time you'll be Mrs David Ross—how does it sound?'

'Perfect!' Laura laughed delightedly. 'Laura Mackenzie Ross… I rather like the sound of that, don't you?'

'I most certainly do. Now I suggest we tell the kids what's happening and then get our skates on and start making plans.' Then David groaned. 'You do realise that this is going to start people gossiping all over again? I can just imagine what Marion Rimmer is going to make of the fact we're getting married at such short notice, can't you?'

'I can, indeed!' Laura laughed. She drew back slightly and there was faint uncertainty in her eyes as she looked at him. 'I almost wish it were true. I would love a child, David, but how do you feel about the idea? Would you mind very much?'

'Mind?' The word came out as a small explosion. He drew Laura back into his arms and held her as though he'd never let her go again. 'I can't think of anything more wonderful!'

'I hoped you'd feel like that.' Laura kissed him with slow thoroughness so that his breathing was ragged when she drew back. She grinned wickedly up at him. 'So, let Marion Rimmer and anyone else say what they like. I might not be pregnant at the moment but who knows what will happen in a few months' time?'

She slipped her hand into David's, her eyes adoring him. 'Let's go tell the kids, shall we? Then we have a wedding to arrange!'

EPILOGUE

SAM O'NEILL brushed the confetti off his jacket before he let himself into the house. David and Laura had taken everyone by surprise by getting married like that, but he didn't blame them. It had been obvious they were crazy about one another so what point would there have been waiting?

He made his way to the tiny kitchen and plugged in the kettle, thinking back over the events of the day. The registry office ceremony had been brief, but everyone present had been touched when the couple had taken their vows with such sincerity. Even he'd felt a bit choked, which had surprised him. Getting married—it certainly wasn't on his agenda!

The kettle came to the boil so he made himself a cup of coffee and carried it through to the living-room. He sat down on the shabby sofa and looked around with a sigh. He'd been renting the cottage for over a year now and had grown quite fond of the place, but it was time to move on.

Africa beckoned—wide open spaces, new challenges, a whole different way of life. The reason he'd steered clear of any personal involvements was because he intended to see his dream come true, and in a few weeks' time that was going to happen.

He would miss Yewdale, of course, and all the friends he'd made here—Abbie in particular—but he'd decided what he'd wanted a long time ago and had planned accordingly. He had no ties, no commitments, nothing and nobody to keep him here. When the time came he could up and leave without a single regret.

Sam picked up his cup and drank a toast to the future.

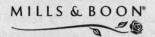

Makes
any time
special

Enjoy a romantic novel from
Mills & Boon®

Presents™ *Enchanted*™ *Temptation*®

Historical Romance™ *Medical Romance*™

MILLS & BOON®

Medical Romance™

COMING NEXT MONTH

MORE THAN A MISTRESS by Alison Roberts

Anna's first House Officer job was in surgeon Michael Smith's hospital. She couldn't believe this was the same man she'd met on holiday, and parted from so badly. And Michael was no happier to see her!

A SURGEON FOR SUSAN by Helen Shelton

Susan was appalled when her sister set her up with a blind date! But Adam had been equally set up, by *his* sister. He was *so* gorgeous, why would anyone think he needed help finding a woman?

HOME AT LAST by Jennifer Taylor
A Country Practice—the third of four books.

After a year away Holly Ross felt able to come home. Many changes awaited her, not least a new stepmother. But the biggest change of all was her growing feelings for Dr Sam O'Neill, the partnership locum.

HEART-THROB by Meredith Webber
Bachelor Doctors

Peter's photo was plastered on *Hospital Heart-throb of the month* posters, embarrassing him when Anna came to work with him in A&E. She was intriguing and mysterious, and Peter couldn't help being fascinated. But he'd managed to stay a bachelor this far...

Available from 2nd July 1999

Available at most branches of WH Smith, Tesco, Asda, Martins, Borders, Easons, Volume One/James Thin and most good paperback bookshops

MILLS & BOON®

Historical Romance™

Coming next month

AN INNOCENT PROPOSAL
by Helen Dickson

Set in 1756

Louisa's brother had just lost their home to Alistair, Lord
Dunstan! Alistair had previously offered her his
protection, but now that her home was at stake she
couldn't refuse him any longer...

MISS JESMOND'S HEIR
by Paula Marshall

A Regency delight!

The second of two books.

Jess Fitzroy infuriated the widowed Mrs Georgina
Herron, and didn't think of her as a suitable *parti* for a
wife, until he learned the truth behind the façade Georgie
presented to the world...

On sale from 2nd July 1999

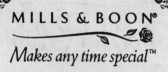

MILLS & BOON®

Makes any time special™

By Request™

Bestselling themed romances brought back to you by popular demand

Each month By Request brings you three full-length novels in one beautiful volume featuring the best of the best.

So if you missed a favourite Romance the first time around, here is your chance to relive the magic from some of our most popular authors.

Look out for
***Her Baby Secret* in June 1999**
featuring Lynne Graham,
Jacqueline Baird and Day Leclaire

FREE
2 BOOKS
AND A SURPRISE GIFT!

We would like to take this opportunity to thank you for reading this Mills & Boon® book by offering you the chance to take TWO more specially selected titles from the Medical Romance™ series absolutely FREE! We're also making this offer to introduce you to the benefits of the Reader Service™ —

★ FREE home delivery   ★ FREE gifts and competitions
★ FREE monthly Newsletter   ★ Exclusive Reader Service discounts
★ Books available before they're in the shops

Accepting these FREE books and gift places you under no obligation to buy; you may cancel at any time, even after receiving your free shipment. Simply complete your details below and return the entire page to the address below. *You don't even need a stamp!*

YES! Please send me 2 free Medical Romance books and a surprise gift. I understand that unless you hear from me, I will receive 4 superb new titles every month for just £2.40 each, postage and packing free. I am under no obligation to purchase any books and may cancel my subscription at any time. The free books and gift will be mine to keep in any case.

M9EC

Ms/Mrs/Miss/Mr ....Initials ....
BLOCK CAPITALS PLEASE

Surname...

Address..

....

....Postcode ....

Send this whole page to:
THE READER SERVICE, FREEPOST CN81, CROYDON, CR9 3WZ
(Eire readers please send coupon to: P.O. BOX 4546, DUBLIN 24.)

Offer valid in UK and Eire only and not available to current Reader Service subscribers to this series. We reserve the right to refuse an application and applicants must be aged 18 years or over. Only one application per household. Terms and prices subject to change without notice. Offer expires 31st December 1999. As a result of this application, you may receive further offers from Harlequin Mills & Boon and other carefully selected companies. If you would prefer not to share in this opportunity please write to The Data Manager at the address above.

Mills & Boon is a registered trademark owned by Harlequin Mills & Boon Limited.
Medical Romance is being used as a trademark.

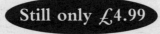